Tales from the Canyons of the Damned

DANIEL ARTHUR SMITH

Tales from the Canyons of the Damned No. 21

First Edition

Special thanks to Jessica West

ISBN-13: 978-1946777522 ISBN-10: 1946777528

Cover By Daniel Arthur Smith

Horror Fiction from Holt Smith ltd
Agroland
Tower

For Susan, Tristan, & Oliver, as all things are.

Captain Sharpteeth
Michael Ezell

EDDY "CHUBS" LANGWORTHY WAS three months shy of his fifteenth birthday when his friend Nate Hammond was horribly murdered.

That's how Eddie's mom put it. "Poor, poor Nate. So horribly murdered."

"Hay-suse on a crutch," Eddie's father had said. "Maria, it's always horrible to be murdered." Larimore Langworthy was a pragmatic man with little patience for dithering about, and always had an opinion on the matter. Every matter.

Whenever he dropped Eddie off to hang out, his dad always eyeballed the Hammonds' sprawling house with that old Langworthy disdain. "The old man's probably mortgaged to the eyeballs to keep that new wife happy."

Like Eddie cared. Mortgages were some nonsense parents worried about. Whatever it cost, Nate had a heated pool. During the fall, ribbons of steam rose off the water, and Nate, Eddie, Rolf Larsen, and Jennifer

Dirickson would pretend they were swimming across that creepy-ass water in front of the door to the mines of Moria. Tall and skinny, Rolf swam like a seal, so he always got a shriek out of Jennifer by diving down and grabbing her ankles.

One of the greatest things about swimming in Nate's pool was that Eddie could swim in his shirt to keep his body covered and no one gave him crap about it. They were his friends; they gave him crap about everything else.

So of course, when Eddie showed up to Nate's wake in a suit jacket that fit like a sausage casing, Jennifer strolled up and said, "What's with the Hulk jacket?"

Probably the smartest person in their school, Jennifer hid a vicious wit behind her perfect GPA, and the bullies at school had learned to avoid her.

"Hilarious," Eddie said. "My mom bought it on sale last month. She gave me too much credit on how much effort I would put into losing weight at camp."

They stood in one corner of the viewing room, surrounded by murmuring adults. Very few people went near the ocean-blue coffin on the pedestal. The casket was closed. Everyone knew why, but no one talked about it.

Jennifer seemed edgy; her gaze flitted about and wouldn't meet Eddie's. She chewed one corner of her lower lip and kept giving him nervous smiles when he caught her.

Nate's parents were nowhere to be seen. Their preacher and an uncle from the mother's side exchanged grim handshakes and pained expressions with guests.

Rolf Larsen, the last member of their fellowship, clip-clopped across the tiles in ridiculous wingtip shoes. His gray suit looked like it belonged to his dad. It was both too large and too old. His white-blond hair rioted atop his head, sticking up every which way.

"I looked everywhere. They're a no-show. You believe his parents aren't at their own kid's wake?" Rolf said.

"Rolf, you're beautiful but stupid," Jennifer said. "Their son was ripped apart by crazed animals or something. They don't want to stand around and listen to people say 'I'm sorry.'"

The three of them fell silent and watched the adults give each other awkward comfort. Sheriff Williams showed up, his white mustache freshly waxed, a shiny badge clipped to his belt, and a threadbare suit jacket hiding his gun. The entire town was in shock, so it probably did the old guy good to remind them that their Sheriff cared. Especially during an election year.

The Sheriff gave them a nod, but didn't come over. Eddie was at camp when it happened, and the Law had already tagged and catalogued the nothing that Jennifer and Rolf knew.

Eddie's mind kept tripping over the last time he saw Nate, the night before camp started. Nate came over and they monitored an eBay auction for a Batman cowl used onscreen by Christian Bale. (Eddie didn't care for the gravelly voice, but Bale had a decent enough chin for the job.) Nate had saved all his allowance to put a bid on the cowl. He worshipped at the church of Batman, wouldn't even entertain a conversation with Superman heretics or, even worse, the unwashed masses who followed Iron Man.

Within five minutes, the price of the cowl soared into the range only adults with no children or social life could afford to pay. Nate left dejected but alive, definitely not shredded and spindled.

The image of Nate waving as he climbed into his dad's Land Rover that night did what the news of his death had not. It made Eddie want to bawl out loud in front of everyone. His chest hitched, but he choked it down before any sound came out. Suddenly, the room stank of old people and new coffins, and anywhere else in the world seemed like a great place to be.

"Let's get outta here," Eddie said.

The staccato sound of their dress shoes echoed back from the storefronts they passed. Taller than Eddie in her bare feet, Jennifer towered over him in heels, making him feel like he was out for a walk with his big sister. At least, he used to feel that way. In the last few months, he had developed a new appreciation for Jennifer's infectious giggle and her flat front teeth that stood out from the others the slightest bit.

They walked for blocks and blocks, Rolf chattering about some new online clan he'd joined and Jennifer needling him with gamer-nerd jokes. To Eddie it was just comforting noise, a distraction from the sealed blue coffin. They veered around the legs of a homeless man who lay curled like a question mark in the doorway of a vacant business.

Rolf stopped in his tracks and gawked at something across the street like Hay-suse just turned up in the crosswalk.

Jennifer let out a little gasp. Eddie tried to figure out what they were looking at, but everything was in soft focus beyond the middle of the street. He got his mother's straight hair and his father's eyesight. Up close was fine, so he never carried his glasses. It was hard enough surviving Middle School as "Chubs." No way he was adding glasses to the mix for High School.

"What's up?" Eddie said.

Rolf and Jennifer didn't answer. They each took an arm and pulled him across the street toward a storefront. A gray mannequin head in a window display wore a Batman cowl. A placard below read: Screen-Used by Christian Bale - Enter Now to Win!

"No way," Eddie said.

The sign above the door had copper letters on black marble.

WELDON'S COLLECTIBLES.

Eddie yanked open the glass door and stepped into the dimly lit store. He heard a distant bing-bong chime somewhere in the back. Jennifer and Rolf crowded in behind him and the trio appeared in miniature on one of the security monitors behind the main counter.

There was something for every collector in the world here. Comic books in plastic sleeves, vases and silver sets, film props, baseball cards, old toys in original boxes. Dozens of shelves, glass cases, and pedestals crammed with shit people loved to hoard.

A wheezy vent overhead blew stale air with an odd, tinny smell to it.

"You think it's the same cowl?" Rolf said. He whispered like they were in church.

Nate had posted his lamentation online after he lost the auction. He got over twenty Likes and Crying-Faces.

"Who knows? There have to be a lot of them out there," Eddie said.

"The air stinks in here. Let's go," Jennifer said.

"Sorry about that."

They all three flinched. Holy shit, where did he come from?

A dude stood behind the counter at the far end of the store, maybe around thirty or so, tall and skinny. Like, unhealthy skinny, with ropy muscles in his arms and pasty skin that hung slack. He smiled with yellowed teeth.

"Hey, it's the Three Musketeers." He looked at Eddie. "You must be Porthos."

"That is actually a new one," Eddie said.

The dude's eyes slid up and down Jennifer without any hint of slyness or apology. "Welcome to Weldon's Collectibles."

"Are you Mr. Weldon?" Rolf said.

"I am indeed Weldon. Don't know that there needs to be a Mister in there. What can I do for you tender young lads and lass?"

Eddie became sharply aware of Weldon's body odor, a musky sour smell like laundry that sat in the washer too long. "A friend of mine tried to buy a cowl like yours on eBay a few weeks ago. Price went too high, though," Eddie said. He nodded toward the window display.

"Yeah, I hate when that happens. But hey, he can enter to win this one for free. It's kind of my way of introducing the store to the community," Weldon said.

"He can't. He's dead," Eddie said.

"Murdered," Rolf added.

Jennifer and Eddie gave him a look.

"What? He was," Rolf said.

"Then he definitely can't enter," Weldon said. "Each entrant has to sign by his own hand."

"Or hers," Jennifer said.

"Sure, by her own slender, lovely hand," Weldon said.

Creepy. Eddie had a vision of Weldon's bony fingers intertwining with Jennifer's and seriously needed to change the subject. "Maybe Nate signed up before he... passed. Could you look it up?"

"What's his last name?" Weldon said.

"Hammond," Eddie said.

"Nope," Weldon said.

"You didn't look," Rolf said.

"To be honest, man, I only have seventeen entries so far. He ain't one of them."

"We should do it, you guys," Jennifer said.

"What would we do with a Batman cowl?" Rolf said.

"It would be kind of like a memorial thing if we win. I don't know, maybe we take a pic with it and leave it at Nate's grave site," Jennifer said.

"Sounds like a noble cause," Weldon said. "This guy must have been a good friend."

"Yeah..." Eddie said. "He was."

"Well, here's where the whole thing might get a little weird," Weldon said. "Depending on your point of view." He knelt and rummaged under the counter for something, revealing a thin spot in the oily hair behind the crown of his head. Jennifer made a gross face and Rolf snickered quietly.

Weldon stood with an odd little smile. "Here we go."

He plunked a large book down on the counter. It had a blue leather cover and was wider than it was tall. It looked like the receipt book the school photographer used. Except when Weldon opened his book, a coppery smelled hit Eddie and made his guts rumble loud enough that everyone glanced at him.

Names and addresses were scrawled in the book, but in boxes alongside the names, there were fingerprints dried to a dark brownish color.

"You seriously have to sign in blood?" Eddie said.

"Ew," Jennifer said.

"Sorry, man. My cowl, my rules. That thing cost me a lot of money, so if I give it away for free, I wanna make sure only the hardest of the hard fanboys get it. No offense," Weldon said. He directed the last at Jennifer with a wet-lipped smile that made her visibly shudder. His smile grew wider.

"Isn't that unsanitary?" Rolf said.

"Nope. Everyone gets their own pricker," Weldon said. He held up three of those little things people on diabetes commercials use to test their blood. "Which one of you dudes wants to show the lady how easy it is?"

That settled the sanitary issue. Rolf picked up the pen to write his name.

While he waited his turn, Eddie noticed Weldon's necklace. A simple piece of black cord with a small head dangling from it. Yellowed and laced with fine cracks, the pendant struck Eddie as something very, very old. The head was about the size of a pecan and had a crude cowl or mask carved into it, but other than that, it seemed to be all teeth.

"What's that?" Eddie said.

"Oh, that's Captain Sharpteeth," Weldon said.

"Captain who?" Eddie said. He honestly wasn't sure he heard. A slight ringing had started in his ears and if he didn't know better, it seemed to be coming from Weldon's necklace...

"Okay, here we go," Rolf said. They all stopped to watch him pop the little pricker against his right thumb. A ruby drop formed and grew fat... Rolf used it to make a bloody thumbprint in the box next to his name. Weldon then tore off a perforated stub of blue paper.

"Here's your number, Skinny Thor. It belongs to you and no one else, non-transferrable," Weldon said. "I'll know if you give it to someone else."

"Sure, okay," Rolf said. He grabbed for the stub, but Weldon pulled it back.

"Non. Transferrable," Weldon said.

In the silence, the wheezy air conditioner blew more tinny air between them. Weldon handed over the stub and Rolf raised his eyebrows at Jennifer and Eddie.

"You up next, Porthos?" Weldon said.

Eddie picked up the pen and scratched his name into the next space.

"Hey, a leftie!" Weldon said. "You ever heard the story of Ehud the Left-Handed?"

Thinking this was somehow working its way around to another fat joke, Eddie showed the bare minimum of interest and kept writing. "Is that from 'The Princess Bride'?"

"Is that from—Holy shit, what are they teaching you kids these days? Ehud was a legendary killer in the Bible, an Israelite who slew a Moabite king named Eglon."

Weldon handed Eddie the pricker and watched him do the blood ritual with way too much interest.

"What's with the left-handed thing?" Rolf said.

"In those days, men wore swords on the left, because they were right handed. The king's guards checked Ehud's left side, but he had a special blade concealed on his right thigh. When he was alone with the king, he gutted that old fat bastard Eglon with his left-handed blade. Spilled the shit right out of his intestines."

"Okay, repugnant," Jennifer said. She always aced Vocab quizzes.

Weldon went still and his beady eyes crawled over Jennifer again. "Repugnant or not, Milady, the moral of the story is to never trust a fucking left-handed guest in your house."

Eddie stood there with his bloody left thumb in the air, waiting for Weldon to laugh, or at least crack his yellow smile. He didn't. He just the tore off the numbered stub.

"You know the drill on this, right?" Weldon said.

"Non-transferrable," Eddie said.

"Porthos was never given enough credit for being smart, in my opinion," Weldon said. He turned his eyes to Jennifer, a familiar place for them to land by now. For the first time, Eddie noticed how big Weldon's pupils were. The black inner disc nearly covered the entire pale green iris. Had they been so big a second ago?

"Milady? Will you join the boys?" Weldon said.

"I guess. For Nate," Jennifer said. When she pricked her thumb, Eddie swore Weldon's rough body odor went up a notch. The creepster practically drooled as he handed over her stub.

"Non-transferrable," Jennifer said.

"Milady knows the drill. She's smarter than the boys," Weldon said. He snapped the book shut and there seemed to be an echo in the deadened room for the first time. Eddie glanced at the window display and for a moment, the precious cowl they'd just signed for in blood looked like a rotting piece of foam rubber. An old movie prop.

"Hey, you guys wanna see something cool?" Weldon said.

The three of them simultaneously mumbled about dinnertime and homework and such. Too late. Weldon ducked out of sight again, presumably to put away his ledger. He popped back up with something in his hands and Eddie instantly hated the thing.

It was only an old cardboard hatbox. But it looked oily at the bottom and had a feeling about it. Like if you were cleaning out your grandma's basement and came across this box, you'd leave it and go back upstairs for a sandwich and some sunlight.

Weldon removed the box top and Eddie's lips actually curled away from his teeth like a dog's. Strong fingers dug into his arm and he was surprised to see they belonged to Rolf. Jennifer had somehow moved away, within a step of the front door.

The thing Weldon took out of the box used to be white. Old as dirt, or maybe older, the leathery hide it was made from had taken on an ivory color, like the tusk of something ancient.

It looked kinda like it was once a superhero cowl. Not a big Batman thing with ears, but plain and snug, like the Flash without the lightning bolts on the side. It had begun to fall apart around the eyeholes and a small split showed in the top.

"What is that thing?" Eddie said.

"If you believe in conspiracy theories and aliens and such, there are those who say this was the cowl of a primeval defender of great temples built by the beings who taught the Aztecs star-charting and mathematics," Weldon said.

"Seriously? It's supposed to be alien stuff?" Jennifer said. She had her hand on the bar to push the door open.

"I said 'if you believe'. Never said I did," Weldon said.

Most of that had gone right past Eddie. Their voices were a murmur behind the quiet hum in his head. Hmmmmmm. Almost like the cowl had some internal power source.

"Go ahead, Porthos, you can touch it," Weldon said.

"Nah," Rolf said. He clung to Eddie's forearm. "Nah."

As repulsed as he was—every bit of him hated that thing—Eddie had to touch it. His fingers ached to feel the texture of it. He raised his left arm, since Rolf was clamped to his right.

The instant Eddie's hand caressed the cowl, nothing was there anymore. The store, Rolf, Jennifer, Weldon the creeper. Gone.

Only the thing existed, the feeling of power, looking through those ragged eyeholes, rushing forward through the jungle, finding screaming prey, beating them with flailing limbs made of bone and sinew, shredding their pleas for mercy with his long, sharp teeth.

"Dude, what's wrong?" Rolf shook him, and it took Eddie a second to realize they were standing on the sidewalk outside the store.

"What?" Eddie blinked, trying to focus. Everything looked fuzzy, even stuff up close.

"Thanks for waiting for us, asshole," Rolf said. He let out a nervous laugh.

"What?" Eddie felt like he was repeating himself. In fact, he knew he was.

"You said, 'I have to go,' and pushed right past me. Are you okay?" Jennifer said.

No.

"Yeah, sure," Eddie said. "We should head back to the funeral home."

His friends gave him odd looks, but they fell in step with him. Rolf asked him about what happened in the store, but Eddie lied and told him he felt sick to his stomach all of a sudden.

When they got back, their parents were pacing outside the funeral home. Eddie's mom had the first emergency text ready to send. Rolf looked to get the worst of it. His dad left when he was three, and his mom was beyond mother-bear when it came to him. Mrs. Larsen's face managed to combine highly pissed off and highly relieved at the same time.

Eddie told them about entering a special raffle in Nate's memory and that knocked the oxygen right out of any potential fire. Children dealing with grief got a pass on wandering away for an hour. (Leaving out the signing in blood bit probably helped.)

Rolf's mom bundled him into the car and Jennifer's parents said their farewells and got the hell out of there. All the adults seemed eager to get this business in their rearview mirrors.

Before the Langworthys could follow suit, Eddie's gut staged a rebellion. His insides had been rumbling like a thunderhead since Weldon opened his damn ledger and the storm finally arrived. No waiting to get home. He had to duck back inside the funeral home. His dad's face contorted to control the embarrassed look, but he covered it by lighting a cigarette. His mom sat in the car and scrolled through her phone.

Entering the side door, Eddie quick-walked a seemingly endless hallway to the back of the building. The restrooms there said Employees Only, but the employees were busy at the moment. If they weren't, too bad, because it was—Time. To. Go.

Bursting into the bathroom like a gunslinger at a saloon, he ran for the lone stall. His head spun with flashes of leafy jungle and rich dark earth and long bony arms striking, crushing. He barely got his pants down in time.

Afterward, when the dizziness and stomach cramps were done, Eddie washed his hands and spent a good five minutes splashing cold water on his face.

The low rumble of men's voices made him freeze. He shut off the water...

The bathroom's frosted window was up about two inches. With his luck, the window opened onto the main parking lot and fifty people had listened to him conduct lengthy splashdown drills. Eddie steeled himself and peeked out the window.

To his relief, a dense screen of bushes stood between the window and a lonely sidewalk leading to a dumpster on the backside of the building. Two men stood there smoking.

One of them was Sheriff Williams. The other man was Father Conway, a stout old priest with white caterpillar eyebrows. Though the Hammonds weren't Catholic, Nate and Rolf had played summer baseball in a league Father Conway put together.

"Lot of people nervous about this one. Animal, you think?" Father Conway said.

Sheriff Williams glanced around to make sure only God and Father Conway were listening. "The Staties are on the case. They don't want us talking about it, but I tell you, Father, this ain't like anything I ever seen. Or heard of. Or read about."

"Yeah... Poor kid. Horribly murdered," the priest said. Like Eddie's mother. He even did the little headshake along with it.

"Naw, sir. Nawwww, sir. He was done in for certain. But that ain't the thing givin' me nightmares. That boy was full as a tick."

"Full? Of what?"

"Human flesh," Sheriff Williams said.

Between the thing in Weldon's store and the Sheriff's sidewalk confessional, Eddie didn't feel much like eating. He pushed his food around, the tines of his fork screeching and scraping against the plate. Scrape, scrape. His mind raced, sprinting through the rich earth and wildflower smells of the jungle. Scrape, scrape, scrape.

"Holy shit, Eddie, enough," his father said.

"Larry!" his mother said.

Unlike most times, Dad actually looked chastened. First off, one did not curse at Marilu Langworthy's dinner table. Secondly, this condition in their son almost certainly revolved around grief over his friend.

Eddie realized his parents were staring at him. "Oh, sorry. What?"

"I said would you like to skip dinner and go upstairs for awhile?" His mother brushed his bangs away from his forehead, which normally irritated the living shit out of him. For maybe the first time ever, he took comfort from it.

"Yeah, if that's okay. I feel kinda... weird."

His father stood and walked behind him. He leaned down and kissed the top of Eddie's head, something he hadn't done since Eddie was in diapers. "It's going to feel weird for a while, son. Losing someone you're close to is a tough thing to deal with."

Eddie retreated to his room before his eyes got too full to blink away the tears. Once he got to his room, though, he kind of lost momentum. He didn't really know what he'd come in there to do, so he sat on his bed and stared at the wall.

Full as a tick.

His father gently knocked on the door and stuck his head in the room. Dealing with all this emotion wasn't Larimore Langworthy's thing. He looked uncomfortable, like he'd mistakenly put on wet underwear.

"Uh... Nate's dad is here. He'd like to speak with you."

The guilty little voice in the back of every kid's head screamed out everything Eddie and Nate had ever done wrong. He imagined his parents and Nate's dad on the living room couch, all looking very stern. We understand you and Nathan were Googling pornography.

Except Mr. Hammond didn't look stern at all when Eddie saw him sitting on the couch. The strong, boisterous guy with graying chest hair who always tossed the kids into the pool looked like a calm breeze might fold him in half. He kept searching for words.

"Nathan is, uh... He was, as you know, Edward, sorry, Eddie, uh... There were things that interested him, that the two of you spoke about." He lurched to a stop.

Eddie glanced at his parents for some divine parental telepathy to tell him what to do. His dad shifted in his seat and cleared his throat. A non-starter, as far as advice goes. His mom inclined her head in Mr. Hammond's direction and raised her eyebrows. Talk to him.

Damn, it worked.

"Yeah, we talked gaming and stuff. Nate loved movie stuff, but you know that," Eddie said. He felt stupid, but something odd happened.

Mr. Hammond straightened up and smiled. "Yes! His collecting of things. I know you weren't into collecting as much as he was, but you know more about it than I do. Could I please ask you to sort his things for me?"

"Sort them?" Eddie said.

"Mazie said there is a children's charity that accepts things for auction. She wants to... Well, we want to donate the real collectible stuff to the charity. Maybe set aside the other things, things he just played with or whatever..." Mr. Hammond trailed off and he sat there taking deep breaths and blinking at the ceiling.

"Yes, I'll help," Eddie said, almost in self-defense. If he leaked so much as a single tear, his mom would swoop on him like a mother hen.

Mr. Hammond found his voice again. "Just you, if it's okay, Eddie. I'm sorry. If the rest of the gang was there, you'd get to talking and I don't think my heart could bear to hear you guys in there without him. Does that seem odd?"

"Not at all," Eddie's mom said.

Maybe to her. The whole damn day had been odd to Eddie. And now he was on his way to separate out his friend's good stuff from the chaff.

Nate's room looked smaller and had the same still air as the funeral home. There were black smudges of fingerprint powder here and there, and everything in the room felt like it had been moved and put back. An array of new cardboard boxes sat on Nate's Darth Vader bedspread. For the "good" stuff. Other boxes near the door were for everyday toys and the like.

Mazie, Nate's step-mom, stayed downstairs, swirling ice cubes in a glass of whiskey and staring off into space. Mr. Hammond had come to the doorway, but no farther, as if a physical barrier of pain kept him out.

Alone, Eddie drifted over to the small desk near the window.

The power indicator on Nate's laptop still blinked, in Sleep mode, as if he just closed it to run down for dinner. (And then somehow wound up in the cold woods, shredded to bits before he could get back to his game or whatever.)

It didn't take Eddie long to box up the collectibles on Nate's shelves. All screen-used, mostly cheap junk. Nate's dad never let him blow too much money on "movie nonsense." There were a couple of nice things, like a Star Trek uniform top worn by Patrick Stewart in First Contact, and one of Rupert Grint's backup wands from Harry Potter.

A quiet thought tickled the edge of his consciousness. The good stuff wasn't out here. His stomach felt slick and bubbly all of a sudden, like it did after he touched the freaky cowl in Weldon's Collectibles.

The folding door to Nate's walk-in closet stood out like a beacon. In there, boy. Treasure be hidden there, fer sher.

Eddie shivered and let out a nervous giggle. That was something Nate always said when they played pirates as kids. They ventured into the woods behind the Hammond house and followed maps Mr. Hammond drew for them. When they arrived at "X", Nate always did his best pirate growl. "Arrr. Treasure be hidden here, fer sher."

And of course, it was. Mainly because Mr. Hammond buried a little bag of quarters or a jar full of candy, something like that.

The knob on the folding closet door felt slippery in his fingers. Eddie tugged it and the door slid open so easy, like it had been waiting for someone to come in. Narrow for a walk-in, and maybe two paces deep. Clothes hung on either side, making the space feel cramped. The air had the smell Mom called "boy-funk."

Eddie didn't bother with the shelves. Nate would never put important stuff up there. Nope, he went to "The Captain's Safe." No one else knew about it, not even Rolf and Jennifer.

Stacks of old video games stood against the back wall of the closet. If you went from top to bottom, it was like excavating the history of X-Box and PlayStation. Taking the game cases together in columns, Eddie shuffled them aside.

This exposed the baseboard along the back section of wall. His fingertips squeezed between the wood and the carpet and lifted up on the board. It moved upward about three inches, the grooved fittings on either end holding it in place.

The first item was expected. An old .22 caliber semi-auto pistol. Tiny, with cheap plastic grips. It had belonged to Nate's grandfather, who most likely never even knew it was gone. Nate snitched it from a rusty toolbox in the old guy's boathouse last summer.

Truthfully, whenever Nate brought the pistol out, the damn thing always made Eddie nervous. It stank of gun oil, and he always worried his mom's famous bloodhound nose would pick it out on his clothes.

He set the pistol aside, unsure if he should chuck the gun in the woods, or turn it over to Mr. Hammond and pretend this was the first time he ever saw it. Maybe the woods thing.

There was something deeper behind the wall, in the dark.

White cardboard peeked out of the blackness. It took Eddie a few moments to work up the nerve to reach for it. A narrow box made of thick cardboard, meant to protect important documents. There was no dust on it, as if Nate had been here recently.

Feeling like a spy who'd been turned against his own side, Eddie opened the box and found 8x10 photo paper stacked face down. He flipped the pictures over and the world took on a different hue.

The first was obviously a cell phone selfie Nate printed out. Jennifer in her bra and jeans, taken in her bathroom mirror. In the next photo, she progressed to her bra and panties.

How long had it been going on? Eddie could imagine Jennifer jumping over a house before he could imagine her sending a pic like this. To anyone. Much less to him, Rolf, or Nate. Her smile felt intimate, like they'd shared these things before. A spark of jealousy quickly turned to guilt. Stupid to be jealous of dead friend. The next pic down, Jennifer had gone without the bra. He quickly snapped that one facedown and took a deep breath. Don't think it, don't think it.

He almost didn't want to look at the next pic. Almost. When he did, Eddie involuntarily let out a low moan. Not in a sexual way. Some animal instinct had made the noise, a primitive reaction to dangerous things.

The picture had been hasty, taken from an awkward angle, but he recognized it anyway. The freaky-ass cowl Weldon kept behind the counter. Nate had seen it in person.

"Weldon, you lying sack of shit," Eddie said.

The air in the closet took on an unpleasant tinny taste.

Treasure, Chubs! Fer sher.

Nate's voice made Eddie flinch. It was just in his head, of course. Yeah, it had to be.

The only time Nate called Eddie by his hated nickname was when he couldn't talk Eddie into doing something, like shooting the little .22 in the woods. "C'mon, Chubs, live a little."

Eddie lurched to his feet and hustled out of the closet. He sat on the corner of Nate's bed, his forehead beaded, flop-sweat staining his shirt. Why would Weldon lie to them about never seeing Nate? Was this something Sheriff Williams should know about? Maybe the Staties, since the Sheriff said they were on the case. They could at least talk to the creepy dude and find out why he denied knowing a murdered kid.

Sitting across from the closet door, the feeling from earlier came back. In there, boy. Treasure be hidden there, fer sher.

If he told himself the truth, which he did not want to do, the feeling never really left. The pictures and the gun were never the treasure. They weren't what Nate wanted him to find. Eddie stared into the shadowy event horizon where the light from the closet ceased and the blackness behind the wall started. Beginning at his wrists, gooseflesh inched up his arms.

Something blue. Small, tucked away where the baseboard corners came together. With another moan he couldn't stop, Eddie shuffled back into the closet. It took a long while, some deep breaths, and calling himself everything nasty name a bully had ever coined before he finally reached in and grabbed the little blue thing.

A piece of paper.

A stub.

"No, no, no." Eddie fumbled through his own pockets and came up with a sweaty bit of blue paper. Nate's was just like it, only fifteen numbers higher. A stub from Weldon's ledger.

To be honest, man, I only have seventeen entries so far. He ain't one of them.

An immediate certainty struck Eddie. Not a notion or a superstitious wondering.

Weldon knew he found Nate's stub.

Non. Transferrable.

Mr. Hammond understood completely when Eddie said he'd have to come back another day and finish. It had all gotten a little overwhelming.

His parents seemed afraid to either intrude or be too distant, so they kind of hovered in Eddie's general direction when he got home. He leaned in and gave them side-hugs, which they were used to, since he was always very body conscious. His vision pulsed in time to his pounding heart. The little .22 pistol felt like a grand piano stuffed in his pocket. He thought for sure any adult who so much as glanced at him would say, "Hey, that kid's got a gun! Get him!"

But he made it to his room without a security pat down and shoved the gun beneath his mattress. He had the photos folded and stuffed in the small of his back under his jacket. He made himself put them next to the gun without looking at Jennifer again.

Pacing his room, his mind spun like a gear that slipped its chain. He opened his laptop and stared at the screen. Where did he even start? He searched for "Weldon's Collectibles."

Nothing. Guy didn't even have an old school web page, much less an interactive site. No Yelp reviews, no mention of him on sites featuring movie collectibles. Eddie gave up and did something he hadn't done since his mom told him about it. He searched for articles on Nate's death. He read several, but not one mentioned what Sheriff Williams talked about.

He tried a search for "full as a tick."

Gross. And not even close to his meaning. No. He sat up straight and gently laid his hands on the keys. He knew what he really meant. Sheriff Williams said that part, too.

Eddie typed in "full of human flesh."

He should've seen the zombie problem coming. Page after page of mostly terrible Halloween zombies eating people. He had to narrow it down. He added "murder victim" and that took him in a different direction.

Most of it was still low budget movie crap, but he found an old link to a story from nineteen years back. It initially read like the crap he saw at the checkout stand when he went to the store with his mom.

ALIENS RUN HOLLYWOOD! CHINA TRAINS DRAGONS FOR NEW ARMY!

One particular headline didn't make him roll his eyes like those others did. It seemed outlandish, sure, but remembering Sheriff Williams' tone of voice, the bold words chilled Eddie like late October.

CANNIBAL VILLAGER EATEN ALIVE!

A junk paper called Inside View claimed to have interviewed the family of a young man in Southern Mexico who was murdered (horribly), but his own stomach was found packed with human flesh. The flesh turned out to be bits of his coworkers.

They all worked for a foreign archaeologist who financed a dig in the jungles where no civilization had been recorded. The locals thought the archaeologist crazy, but the elders said people thought to be insane were sometimes talking to the gods.

The tabloid reporter hadn't bothered to track the facts of the occurrence. He was after the sweet juice running from deeply wounded family members. He interviewed the weeping mother, even included a picture of her lined face stretched into a topographical map of grief.

"He was a good boy. What they say is not true. He would never eat his friends," she said in the actual column.

Beneath her picture, however, the writer put in the caption: Cannibal's Mom says he wouldn't eat those he knew.

The family's home was burned in retaliation and they barely escaped with their lives. "Fleeing into the hostile night," as the writer put it. There was an In Memoriam picture at the end. A group of four workers leaned on their shovels for a moment in the jungle as the rest of the dig continued behind them. The cannibal in question had one of those highlight ovals around his face and the rest of the picture was a bit darker. It was frustrating, because Eddie wasn't interested in the highlighted man. The white man in a waist-deep hole behind the workers captured his attention. The man had one hand on a stone pillar they'd uncovered. He was glancing over his shoulder in annoyance at the men who leaned on their shovels.

Nah. No way.

The archaeologist in the picture couldn't be Weldon. The collectible shop owner was too young. Eddie's paranoia probably had his brain wanting to see some resemblance...

His phone buzzed in his pocket and he nearly wet himself. Happy to shut down the laptop and think about something else, he grabbed the phone.

A text from Jennifer:

—How r u?

—K, I guess...

—What's wrong?

Self-pity welled up, jealousy that she'd shared intimacy with Nate, but not him.

—Nate's dad asked me to sort his stuff. Found pics you might want back. Nate printed and hid in closet.

It took a long time for Jennifer to answer, but she was typing, typing, typing. Probably erasing and starting over a few times.

—I'm embarrassed I sent them, okay? Stupid thing we did over summer. I can't believe he printed them!

Several embarrassed-face emojis followed, interspersed with angry faces.

Now Eddie was at a loss. While he tried to compose a cool way to tell his friend it was no big deal he saw her boobs, the phone buzzed in his hand and a text from an Unknown Number popped up at the top of his screen.

—Porthos! Gimme a buzz, buddy.

Eddie flinched and his phone flew out of his hands. It slid across his bed and fell between the mattress and the wall. It buzzed back there, a hollow drumming against the drywall. Jennifer or Weldon?

He retrieved the phone like he was fishing a cobra out of its hole. Another text from the unknown number waited.

—I'm a little disappointed. It seems you've taken possession of someone else's ticket. Non-transferrable.

The certainty about Weldon knowing had proven true. This guy wasn't just creepy. Something about him tasted like nightmares and oily hands wrapped around a throat.

Eddie typed confident words, but his fingers trembled the whole time.

—Taking it all to police. You knew Nate!

His phone rang immediately. Unknown Number. He didn't want to answer. He wanted to reject the call and do exactly what he texted. Call Sheriff Williams.

C'mon, Chubs. Live a little.

His thumb hit the green circle and he immediately regretted it.

Rolf's voice mewled out of the speaker. He sounded like a little boy who'd lost his way in the dark. "Eddie? My mommy, Eddie. So many teeth. Hit her and bit her..."

Weldon's voice came on. "Come down to the store and bring your ticket. You're the lucky winner, Chubs. Oh, and invite Milady along."

"How? Our parents will never let us go out tonight," Eddie said. In the face of all he'd discovered, real world concerns like curfews and parental control felt like a safe harbor. As long as he didn't sail out into the chop, he'd be okay.

"What, you never snuck out your window? C'mon, Chubs. Live a little."

Up until that point, Weldon's voice had the same light, smartass tone he took with them in the store. Now, it dropped lower, filled with gravel and grinding bones.

"Your friend will die a horrible, shrieking death and then I'll come for your mommy, too. You and the girl, no one else. Hurry along, Eddie."

A sound came out just before the phone went dead. Eddie preferred to think it was Weldon making some weird, high-pitched squeal and not Rolf. He knew he was lying to himself.

He got up and went to tell his parents goodnight. When his kissed his mom's cheek, her perfume almost made him burst into tears. Hopefully they took his hasty exit as one more manifestation of grief.

They never came in his room after he went to bed, so he didn't even make a movie-kid attempt to stuff pillows under his blankets. He'd never dressed for something like a rescue mission before. He settled for a dark blue hoodie with silk-screened image of Willie Nelson on it. His grandmother sent it for his birthday. You like music, right?

Chivalry demanded he leave Jennifer out of it. On the other hand, as Weldon had noted, she was a Musketeer. He sent her a text. While he waited for an answer, he checked Weldon's texts again.

They were gone. So was the incoming call record.

It was almost too easy. Jennifer's parents were also in the stage of leaving their moody teenager to herself once she retired to her room. Besides, she was the original good girl, never snuck out once in her life.

She had the driver pick up Eddie three blocks from his house. Her parents gave her an account with a safe indie ride service for emergencies, and this pretty much constituted an emergency. Whatever was about to happen, the late-night charge showing up on the account would be the least of their worries. They rode in silence, neither acknowledging the pictures nor what they were heading toward. Jennifer's eyes were red and puffy. She loved Rolf's mom, a clever woman with a quick wit and dazzling smile.

The driver thought they were crazy, but he let them off in the neighborhood where Weldon had his store. Once the guy drove away, Eddie's resolve wavered a bit and he stood there in the dark. He felt a warm hand take his, fingers intertwined, giving him strength.

He gave Jennifer a weak smile and they strode down the sidewalk hand in hand. They stepped around a homeless man sleeping under a ratty blanket. The guy smelled like Uncle Mort after a twelve-pack of PBR, and he was snoring lightly. It was too dark to tell if it was the same guy from their first visit to the store.

As they passed him, the snoring stopped. A drunken, slurred voice whispered from beneath the ratty blanket. "Careful, Ehud. This ain't no man you seek to kill."

"Did you hear—" Eddie said.

"No, I didn't," Jennifer said.

They ran across the street, still holding hands. The door to Weldon's Collectibles stood ajar about half an inch. Inside, the store was completely dark.

Jennifer squeezed Eddie's hand. Once. Twice.

He yanked the door open and they stepped inside. The door shut behind them, but no locks clicked into place. On impulse, he reached for it and found it immobile, solid as a pyramid.

The security screens behind the counter winked to life, flooding the room with silvery-blue light. Jennifer and Eddie look like ghosts on one of the screens. All the screens rolled with snow for a second then snapped to an image that made Jennifer gasp.

Nate was on every screen. He wasn't just touching the weird cowl Weldon kept under the counter, he stroked it like a favorite pet. Nate glanced up at the security camera and Eddie's hand rose in a half-hearted wave before he could stop it.

All the images of Nate froze and Weldon's voice came out of the darkness. "Your friend really loved that thing. He wouldn't leave me alone about it, wanted to wear it in the worst way."

Appearing from the back, Weldon carried a knife loosely in one hand. It had a long, thin blade. Eddie went fishing at camp, so he knew a gutting knife on sight.

Weldon seemed to glide forward into the bluish light of the monitors. He wore a dark windbreaker with the hood pulled tight around his face. "The mask provokes unbridled fear in most, but to some...Well, it speaks to them. Whispers about the power. Spoke to you, Porthos, I knooooow it did. Old Captain Sharpteeth showed you his magic."

Jennifer stared at Eddie, but he ignored her, tried not to think of streaking through the jungle, hunting for something to destroy—

Weldon was still talking. "I let your friend wear it. Man, did I ever. Sometimes I like to see all that raw power from the outside." He leered at Jennifer. "I guess you might say I'm a bit of a voyeur."

He stepped through a gap in the counter and the sharp edges of the little .22 pistol's grip bit into Eddie's left palm. He hadn't even thought of reaching for the gun, must've done it on pure instinct. Weldon gave him an odd little grin. It brought back Eddie's paranoia that everyone knew about the gun.

"I chose his prey," Weldon said. "I don't think he would have, had he really known what happens when you put it on. The poor girl was waiting for her boyfriend to pick her up after work. She might have been a little homely to be sacrificed to a demigod, but old Nate... he thought she was mmm-mmm good!"

Full as a tick.

"Why did you kill him?" Eddie said.

"Oh, I didn't. Not in any spiteful sense," Weldon said. "It was just my turn to wear it. You see, Captain Sharpteeth, he doesn't much care if you're friends or family or screwing each other. When he comes to visit, all things are consumed."

"Then why didn't Nate consume you?" Eddie said.

Weldon giggled and wagged the long knife like a razor-sharp finger. "Ah, ah, Chubs. Don't get too curious."

A shrill whistling on the razor edge of human hearing range struck Eddie again. He glanced at Jennifer, but saw no signs she heard it. The last time they came in. Same thing. A low whistling he chalked up to his panic attack. It seemed to come from the tiny head around Weldon's neck—

"Wanna see your friend in action?"

Weldon held up a little remote in his other hand. The images on the screen changed to something Eddie was only too happy to see in poor resolution. A blurred image of long, long teeth and wild eyes with pupils like broken black egg yolks. The only way Eddie knew it was Nate under the leathery, slippery cowl was the tee shirt: a montage of DC villains Nate had bought last year. Behind the sharp teeth and broken-yolk eyes, a red-haired girl had her mouth frozen in a scream apparently only Nate and Weldon ever heard. She was already streaked with blood, and had several long gouges in her cheeks.

"Oh my God," Jennifer said.

"Demigod, really. Created when a minor god lay down with a human woman to breed guardians, someone to watch their backs as they slumbered, you see? Wearing the essence of the guardian is an honor," Weldon said.

Skin. It's made of some alien skin, Eddie thought.

"Oh my God," Jennifer said again. Her voice trembled and tears poured down her face.

Eddie realized she wasn't looking at the screens and followed her terrified gaze. His stomach clenched and threatened to betray him when he saw it. While Weldon pontificated on gods and honor, a figure of horror lurched through the gap in the counter behind him. Covered in blood from head to toe, hands tied in front, ragged bits of flesh hanging off here and there. The only recognizable thing was the white-blond riot of hair.

"Holy shit, Rolf," Eddie managed. He puked all over a display of antique bottle openers.

Weldon spun around and slashed Rolf across his bloody chest. Rolf didn't even flinch. Apparently, the pain he'd already suffered couldn't be topped by a mere slash. His bound hands reached for Weldon's throat, but they were slick with blood and the wiry man squirmed away. He spun the gutting knife into an icepick grip—

The little .22 hammered out thunderclaps inside the shop, not at all like the sharp cracks it made in the open woods. In the dark, Eddie's fuzzy vision was all lights and shadows past ten feet. He held the blurry sights on the shadow he thought was Weldon and jerked the trigger over and over. Jennifer screamed, long and loud, the entire time the gun went off.

Right at the end, something good and something bad happened.

Weldon screeched and dropped the knife.

Rolf let out an awkward squawk and sat down flat on his butt. He looked up at everyone in surprise as a maroon geyser shot out of the little hole in his throat. He fell sideways and twitched a couple of times. Then it was over.

Eddie screamed this time. In rage, fear, and guilt. He threw the empty gun at Weldon, but missed by a good three feet. Even with a hand clasped to his bleeding bicep, Weldon still managed to laugh.

"Lordy, Porthos, don't they teach throwing at Fat Kid Camp?"

Weldon used his good hand to reach inside his windbreaker. "Let me show you what the Masters left behind for us, the thing that makes me rise above all you animals."

He pulled the cracked, yellowed cowl from inside his windbreaker. He smiled and raised it to his head—

Jennifer slammed into him like a linebacker someone forgot to block. The shock on Weldon's face would have been comical if he weren't about to horribly murder them.

With what he hoped was a terrifying battle cry, Eddie leapt into the fight. He and Jennifer rained wild, schoolyard-scuffle blows down on Weldon. Unfortunately, neither Eddie nor Jennifer knew jack shit about fighting. All bones and tough sinew, Weldon threw them off in different directions. Eddie caught a good jab in the face that made his eye throb and swell.

Scrabbling on her hands and knees, Jennifer managed to get hold of the gutting knife. Weldon caught her wrist as she turned and twisted the blade out of her grip. Without hesitation, he gave her a vicious slash, flaying her cheek open in a crescent grin. She fell to the floor and raised her arms to ward him off. Weldon cut her twice across her right forearm.

Eddie moved toward them, but... Something warm brushed against his hand. The cowl. His face went slack and his fingers practically crawled to the thing on their own. He picked it up, caressed it.

Weldon raised his knife like a sacrificial dagger, the killing blow aimed for Jennifer's heart—He suddenly screamed like he'd been hit with boiling water, even though no one had touched him.

Weldon's screech jerked Eddie out of his reverie and he saw what Jennifer had done.

She ripped the tiny ivory head with its long teeth off of Weldon's neck. The strange whistling thing Eddie couldn't get out of his head. Overseers. It protected the Overseers. How the hell did he know that?

The broken cord hung loose from Jennifer's open palm, stuck in the blood on her forearm.

"Give me that, you fucking cunt!" Weldon screamed. His voice went up so high it broke on the last word.

Eddie stood with the old ragged cowl in his hand. "Let her go, Weldon."

Weldon's lips curled from his teeth in a wild dog sneer—which changed completely when he saw what Eddie held.

"Hey, hey, hey," Weldon said. "Easy with that, kid."

Jennifer's voice sounded so small and faraway, her words took a few seconds to register. "He's afraid, Eddie."

Weldon laughed. "You think I'm afraid of Fat-Ass, here? You a fighter, Porthos?"

"He's afraid you'll put it on," Jennifer said.

Without warning, Weldon spun and stabbed her, deep in the belly. He grabbed for the whistling thing in her hand.

Jennifer fought the creepster, even with his knife slicing her insides. She threw the necklace across the shop, into the darkness where it really belonged. Weldon yanked his bloody blade out and pulled Jennifer's hair to expose her throat.

No thought was required on Eddie's part.

The cowl settled around his scalp, snug around his eyes, his suddenly all-seeing eyes.

The one with the blade in its hand stopped trying to cut the bleeding one. It tried to defend itself, but that was truly a jest among demigods. Captain Sharpteeth knew the cold blackness of space, the harsh grind of centuries. A manmade blade held no power over him.

Slashing, tearing, bony arms and sinewy muscle slamming blows against the thin human skull. A raging thirst for blood, sweet shredded tissue stuck between his teeth, his long, gnashing teeth. Full? He could never be full enough. These intruders, destroyers, desecrators, he would consume them all.

The one with the blade had turned into splintered bones and flaps of meat. Boring.

Now his vision, his crystalline clear vision, turned to the bleeding, screaming one. They always screamed. They always begged.

"Eddie, pleeeease! Don't kill me. Eddiieeeee!"

Strong hands gripped his head! Struggling, pulling, tearing away—

It took Eddie a full minute of blinking and shaking his head to understand the hands were his own. He had taken off the cowl. It trembled in his hands like a living thing, a warm, bloodthirsty companion...He threw it into the shadows and crawled to Jennifer.

Her eyes were all whites, all fear. He held out empty hands. "It's me, It's me. We need to call an ambulance for you," he said.

She reached for his hand finally, and pulled him close, searching his eyes. "What was it, Eddie? Where did you go? It was...teeth and bones and..."

Eddie had his phone out, trying to dial with one hand. So much blood, the smell of it, the sticky feel of it all over his face...

Jennifer's hand spasmed and squeezed him hard. "Hurry, Eddie."

He squeezed back. "Stay here. Just stay awake. You're gonna be okay."

A woman's voice came from the phone. "9-1-1 Emergency, what are you reporting?"

"My friend has been stabbed. We need an ambulance. Hurry!" Eddie said. He gave her their location and hung up. He held Jennifer's head in his lap and whispered to her about the school choir not having enough tall girls, so she couldn't die. Her tiny smile made him feel like a victorious gladiator.

He tried not to think about the story he'd have to tell the police shortly. They wouldn't believe him, of course. But later, Sheriff Williams would believe him. No doubt about it.

Because Eddie was full. Full as a tick.

A Cookie Cutter Story
Will Swardstrom

"HEY MEG. YEAH…I…I HOPED I'd catch you before…before I have to do this. I'm going to make things better for us. I know I screw up. I know. Even if you never want anything to do with me again, I'm going to make things right. You won't have to worry, if everything goes right. If…okay. Yeah, sorry babe. Gotta run. I'll call you again later."

He hated leaving a voicemail, but Tyrone Walters didn't have any choice. He shoved the phone into his jeans pocket, but kept the Bluetooth earpiece pressed firmly into his ear.

"Let's go, T!"

The van pulled up in front of an old two-story farmhouse, their de facto leader Jeremy Cross at the wheel. He craned his neck to look back at Tyrone with a mix of pity and disgust. "Look, we're here for a job, not for you to get back in Megan's pants. You here for the right reasons?"

A hand reached back from the front passenger seat and grabbed Jeremy's knee. "Cut him some slack, Jer. It isn't like you don't want to inspect my shorts after we're done, right?"

The hand belonged to Liv Tippy, Jeremy's current squeeze. Current, Tyrone thought, because in the girlfriend department, Jeremy tended to have a revolving door. Liv had actually managed to last for the past five months, almost unheard of in Jeremy's world.

Annoyed, Tyrone didn't give Jeremy a chance to answer Liv. "Yeah, Jeremy. I'm good."

"That's what I like to hear!" a voice practically shouted from the back seat and a big hand clapped down on Tyrone's shoulder. Tyrone winced at the sudden pressure and smiled. Frank Cassel was a large man, and always up for a little mayhem. He took his name to heart and embraced the comic book character aspect, wearing black all the time and Punisher t-shirts whenever he could get away with it.

Frank shifted his attention from Tyrone to Jeremy. He pounded the seat in front of him, and asked, "So what's the deal with this house again?"

"Geez. I told you twice already," Jeremy said.

Frank glared at him. Tyrone tensed up, knowing that Jeremy liked to goad Frank, knowing that the large man rarely took the bait. Frank instead paused, and spoke with an even, perhaps even jovial tone.

"So tell me again. You know all those concussions I had in high school haven't exactly helped my long term memory. Besides, I like to hear about an easy mark again and again."

Jeremy seemed on edge, hesitant...until Liv ran her hand up his leg again. "Come on, babe. Tell us again what you found."

The leader of their little band of thieves cracked a sly smile. "Yeah, okay, so last week I got a call from Rick Olson. Said the family of this old lady wanted us to run an estate sale for them. Kicker is that they're all out of state and can't be here until next week. We're supposed to get everything ready for the day of the sale and they just show up. The old lady's been dead a few months now, and they need to get the house empty and sold as soon as possible, they said. So I come out the other day with Rick," Jeremy paused for effect, "and this place is just packed. Floor to ceiling, there's nothing but quality stuff in there. Loads of jewelry, antique silverware, and all sorts of little trinkets we can get out of there without anyone even noticing. Best part is this house is miles away from anybody. Perfect crime."

Jeremy clapped his hands and grinned maniacally. Tyrone felt his stomach flip, but it always did on a job like this. Hopefully this would be the last one. Tyrone needed it to be the last one. He'd help this last time, but he needed a score of his own so he and Meg could start their lives comfortably...if she took him back, that is.

"Well, hot dog, what are we waiting for?" Frank shouted. He reached around Tyrone and pulled the door open then ran ahead towards the old farmhouse. Tyrone pulled himself out and stood for a moment outside the van, just staring down the turn-of-the-century home. Liv put a hand on his arm.

"You okay, T?"

Tyrone looked down at Liv. She was small, almost too small to even be called petite, but she made up for it with attitude.

"Yeah. I guess," he said. "I just don't have a good feeling about this. It all seems too good to be true."

Liv followed Tyrone to the house. The awning seemed to tilt and sway with the soft breeze. She leaned in close and talked to him as if they were the only two there. "It'll be okay, T. Look, you go and do your thing. Pick any locks we need you for, and then you can just go back to the van if you want. Cool?"

Tyrone shook his head. The full moon overhead let him see the expression on Liv's face, but Tyrone wasn't going to show any weakness in front of Jeremy and Frank. They were already waiting by the front door. Tyrone did his best to shake off his hesitation.

"Nah. I'll be fine. Let's move."

Tyrone followed Jeremy, Liv, and Frank down the main hallway of the old homestead. Unlike modern houses with their wide open floorplans, this house was divided into a collection of rooms. Each room had its own doorway off the main artery. Jeremy directed each member of the team to a different room to start their search for treasures small enough to carry but large enough to matter. Tyrone was picked last. They sent him to the kitchen.

He entered the room, careful to leave his fingertips on his small flashlight instead of the light switch. No need to leave any extra prints, just in case something tipped off the family or the authorities. Tyrone pushed the button on the bottom of the LED flashlight and immediately illuminated the room from floor to ceiling. The kitchen was remarkably clean, but on every level surface there were cookie jars, plates, dishes of every sort and size, a few pots and pans, silverware, and every odd or end that one might expect to find in a farmhouse kitchen.

He scanned the housewares, looking for the right score. He saw a box on the edge of the table, and reached down to grab it.

"Hey, Tyrone!"

Liv strode into the room with a zeal unfit for a late-night robbery.

Tyrone jumped a couple inches, then straightened up and glowered at her. "Yeah?"

"I was just checking to see what you got there," she said. She pouted a little at his tone.

"I don't know. I just started. I'll let you know after I finish up. Why don't you go find Jeremy and tell him what I've found so far. That's what he sent you to do, isn't it?"

Liv took another step into the kitchen, her mouth slightly open.

"Of course not," she said after a moment's hesitation.

Tyrone smirked. "Whatever. I've known Jeremy for too long. Hell, you'll be gone in a couple weeks. He's all about the cheap thrills."

Liv stamped a foot on the aged linoleum. "I ain't cheap!"

"Never said you were," Tyrone said. He left the unsaid implication hanging. Liv's eyes widened and she stared Tyrone down in the light from the LED. She smacked the door frame next to her. "You're a prick when you want to be. You know that? I was nice to you outside."

She flicked on her own flashlight and stormed off. Tyrone breathed a sigh of relief. If he was going to make this his last job, he didn't need any distractions, especially with a little trifle like Liv. He had his own worries with Meg.

Remembering Meg, he tried calling again, but the call went to voicemail. He didn't want to seem desperate, but he didn't want to leave a hang-up on a message, so he hung on until after the beep.

"Yeah. Hey Meg, it's me again. I know you said you were going out tonight with your girlfriends, so I wasn't expecting you to pick up, but if you did, I wouldn't be mad. Uh, not that I have any right at all to be mad. You…you're the only one with that right, I guess. I'd like to fix what I did wrong. I think I may be able to after tonight. I've got a little work to do. I'll call you later. Love you…"

Tyrone hung up and admired the box, working it over with his hands. He tried to pry it open with his fingernails, but nothing was giving. It was exquisite, clearly wooden, but smooth as any metal, extremely heavy for its size, hinged, with a lock on its front clasp. Whatever was in here was something valuable. Extremely valuable. Tyrone just needed to figure out how to open it.

A few doors down the hall, Frank Cassel stepped into a sewing room. Piles of fabric everywhere buried any potential hidden treasures. He sighed, knowing the chances of finding anything worth pawning were remote at best. But unwilling to give up, he took a few steps farther into the room. That's when he noticed a few embroidery samplers—intricately stitched and framed— lining the walls.

Frank swore under his breath. These might actually be worth something, but he couldn't take them all. He stepped closer to the first one on his right to get a closer look. He went from one to another, gleaning what he could about each one so he could tell Jeremy and Tyrone about them.

The first—a simple alphabet. A sampler, if his memory was correct. The next—the Lord's Prayer. From one to the next, they offered simple sayings a farmhouse might display.

But the last one caught Frank's attention. While the words were clearly legible, they were also cryptic and strange. Frank didn't know what they meant, but he figured Tyrone would. If anyone in the house would know, it would be T. Frank grabbed the frame off the wall and tucked it under his arm. He went to see what his friend thought of the piece.

Liv sauntered into an upstairs bedroom where she found Jeremy Cross rifling through the nearest chest of drawers. His left arm was already decorated with several necklaces and bracelets. When he saw her walk in, he straightened up.

"Hey, Livvy Love. What're the others up to? They stuffing their own pockets first?"

"Who cares?"

Jeremy felt his blood pressure rise. This wasn't part of the plan. He wasn't about to let Liv wreck his evening.

"What do you mean, who cares?"

Liv dropped onto the bed in the middle of the room. "I mean, I'm not a snitch. You wanna find out what Tyrone and Frank are doing, you do it. If you didn't bring guys you can trust, then why bring them at all?"

Jeremy paused for a moment, considering how to massage the situation. He sat down next to Liv, putting his arm around her shoulders. "Look Liv, I'm doing this for you. For us, really. If this old lady was loaded, then we could make some bank here tonight. I trust Tyrone. We've been friends since the first day of high school. I trust Frank, even if he is a massive dick sometimes. In the last few months, I've really come to care about you and I just wanted you to feel like you were a part of the team."

Liv sniffled and leaned away from him. "No you didn't. You don't care about me. Tyrone says you'll dump me in a couple weeks and move on to another girl."

Jeremy silently cussed Tyrone then said to Liv. "Tyrone is wrong. I would've left you at home if that was the case. Instead, I wanted you here. I wanted to make you a partner tonight. Whatever we get tonight, you're getting a quarter of it. I promise."

The sniffling stopped and Liv turned her face up toward Jeremy's. Her pleading eyes softened anything inside of him. "Really?"

"Really. I promise."

In a flash, she stood up and pushed Jeremy down on the bed. She straddled him and pulled her shirt off.

"Prove it. Here. Now."

Tyrone was frustrated. He'd been looking around the kitchen for a key to the lock on the polished wooden box. Whatever was inside was clearly worth taking, but Tyrone knew Jeremy would want to know what it was before they just took the whole thing.

"Yo, T!"

Tyrone swiveled with a start, once again not expecting a voice behind him in the old creaky farmhouse. He sighed, seeing Frank in the doorway. At least it wasn't Liv again, spying on him for Jeremy. The big lug had some picture in a frame or something.

"Yeah. What's up?"

"Look what I found. I think it's really interesting."

Tyrone smirked. There were a great number of things could be interesting to Frank, very few of which would actually bring any cash at the pawn shop.

"Yeah. Why don't you put it down on the table over there and I'll look at it in a minute. I'm looking for a key," Tyrone said. He turned back to the cabinets and drawers lining one of the kitchen walls.

As Frank put the sampler on the table, he saw the box. "You looking for a key to this box?"

Tyrone didn't look up as he rifled through a junk drawer. "Yep."

Frank spotted a meat tenderizer in a utensil crock on the counter. "We don't need no key. Check this out."

Tyrone turned around just in time to see Frank swinging the meat hammer down onto the lock. The first swing didn't fix Tyrone's problem, but when Frank encountered an obstacle like this, he wouldn't stop until he won or destroyed the entire kitchen—whichever came first.

Whack. Whack. Whack.

A few blows later, the lock popped open. The box suffered a bit in the process, but Tyrone didn't care. He had already determined the prize lay not in the packaging, but the goods within. If the money he could get from whatever was inside the box proved to be enough, he and Meg could live happily ever after. Tyrone took the meat tenderizer from Frank before the huge man could do any more damage.

"Good job, Punisher. I think you got it."

Frank grinned at the nickname, and smoothed down his black and white skull T-shirt.

Tyrone carefully pulled the lock off the box and flipped open the clasp. He pushed the top open…only to discover a smaller metal box inside. He tried it as well. Closed. No key to be found.

"Dammit."

Before Tyrone could say anything else, Frank reached around him and grabbed the metal box. He lifted it over his head and threw it down on the floor. The lid popped open and spilled its contents under the table.

"Frank!"

The giant of a man looked confused by Tyrone's rebuke at first, then apologetic. "Sorry. I'll help you pick it up."

Reaching under the table, Tyrone located the metal box. Peering inside, he saw indentations reserved for four shapes. A solitary cookie cutter remained in the box. The bigger female shape. The Mother. The kind people used to make gingerbread cookies before the holidays. He instantly flashed on Meg. Last Christmas, they had taken a day and made a few dozen gingerbread men for a bake sale at the hospital she worked for. Half of them ended up going to kids in the Oncology unit as fast as she could sneak them in. He smiled, remembering the pictures she'd shown him later. The smile disappeared as he realized the expensive loot he was expecting in the box was a set of gingerbread people.

"What the heck?" Frank exclaimed. He sat up, holding a little girl cookie cutter. With the Mother, they had two of the family of four. "Wait…I think I see another one." He reached over and grabbed a second shape and put both in the box before he stood up. It was dear old Father cookie cutter. Tyrone shone his light around the kitchen, but didn't see any others.

"This is what you were desperate to see?" Frank asked.

"Well…I…uh…There was a lock on the box! Wouldn't you have tried to get into it, too?"

Frank scrunched his mouth and bobbed his head up and down. "I guess? You got me there. Hey, let's take a look at this sampler I found in the other room. I think it was the only interesting thing in there."

Tyrone took one last look at the three cookie cutters before pushing the box to the far side of the table. Frank handed him the frame. He'd seen tons of these in antique stores, but no one wanted them anymore. They were a dime a dozen. It was as much of a bust as his silly cookie cutters. He told Frank as much.

"But read the words. All the others were little prayers or the alphabet, but this one's different!"

Tyrone squinted a little in the low light and had to agree. The words were unique as far as samplers went. This one read like a two-verse poem of sorts. It begged to be read aloud, so he started reading the lines.

"Late in the night they rise as one
Pieces of tin, when called they run
...If you see them,
Beware. Beware the curse...Can you catch them?
Take care. Beware the verse.

Saying these Words will Make It Done
Father, Mother, Daughter, and Son
The family of four. Alive! They come.
The frolic of imps, the rogues of fun."

While he read, Tyrone felt the entire house fall silent around him, as if everything around him held its breath while it waited for him to finish. It seemed almost reverent.

A couple seconds after he finished, Tyrone heard a metallic clink on the far side of the kitchen. He swung his flashlight around and shone it against the wall. Nothing there. Another clink near the doorway. Frank aimed his light there. Nothing.

More and more metallic clinks and the kitchen became a hive of activity. Neither Tyrone or Frank could find what was going on with their small lights, but on the last sweep with his flashlight, Tyrone glimpsed the cookie cutter box. A few minutes earlier, it held three small shapes. Now it was empty.

"Dude. What happened?" Frank said.

In the bedroom upstairs, Jeremy had completely forgotten about picking the house over for antiques and collectibles. The vision before him was even greater than trinkets and baubles. Liv's smooth skin seemed to glow in the dimly-lit room.

He lay back on the bed, fixated on the thin bra holding Liv's pink breasts in front of him. "You sure about this?"

Liv bent down, her body pressing against his. She whispered in his ear, "You're the boss. You tell me. What's more important—the job or me? Choose wisely."

Jeremy didn't ponder his situation long. The urging below took control. He maneuvered around and began to kiss and caress Liv's body. His hands had a mind of their own as they explored her mostly bare torso, stopping briefly along her back to unclasp her bra. Once accomplished, they moved back around to the front to free the beauties, as he liked to call them.

Liv wasn't ready for him to take total control. She put her mouth on his and explored with her tongue. Everything she did was driving him wild with anticipation.

Suddenly, she twitched and jerked.

"Stop it," she murmured. She didn't stop kissing him, but playfully slapped his chest.

He wasn't sure what she meant, but he was willing to play along. "Stop what?"

She twitched again. "You've already unhooked my bra. Stop tickling me." Another spasm, but this time she sat up. "I'm serious. If you don't want to do this, then we'll stop."

"What are you talking about? My hands are right here," Jeremy argued, showing her that he'd been working on getting her pants off the whole time.

Liv froze.

"Then. What. Is. On. My. Back?"

She slowly looked around and a glint of metal flashed in the near darkness. Jeremy grabbed it. He pushed Liv back on the bed and slammed the object to the floor. He was glad he still had his boots on when he jumped off the bed and stomped on the thing a few times until he was confident it was dead.

"What was that?" Liv asked.

"I dunno. A mouse? A rat? Never can tell in a house like this."

"Shut up. You know that isn't what it was. Shine your phone down there. Let's see." Liv was still shaking, but hadn't put her shirt back on yet.

They sat on the edge of the bed and Jeremy pulled his phone out of his front pocket. Liv leaned forward to see for herself. What they saw shocked Jeremy into silence. Liv, however, screamed.

"Did you hear that?" Frank asked Tyrone.

"I sure did. Let's go."

They took the stairs two at a time, reaching the top in seconds. They found Jeremy and Liv perched in the middle of a large bed in the first bedroom to the right. They were hesitant to enter, seeing Liv without a shirt. Tyrone considered to himself that perhaps the scream was part of…whatever the two of them were doing.

"Uh…are you guys…Should we come back?" Tyrone offered.

"NO!" they said in unison.

"Hey, uh, Liv…" Frank started, and then gestured at his chest. She looked down and saw her breasts swinging free from a loose bra. Her cheeks flushed. In less than a minute, she'd put her shirt back on, but not before she started to tell their story.

"There's something on the floor. I thought Jeremy killed it. He might have. I don't know. Tell them, Jeremy," Liv said.

Jeremy didn't say anything. Tyrone thought he looked like he'd seen a ghost.

"Forget Jeremy, Liv. What'd you see?" Frank asked.

"Well, look down there. See for yourself!" she cried.

Frank and Tyrone looked at each other and then back at Liv. Tyrone hesitantly shone his light down at the floor. There was nothing. A few scratches on the wood.

"There's nothing down there," Tyrone said.

"What do you mean?" Liv exclaimed. "Jeremy flattened it, and there were three others. We just saw them and it looked like a whole family of…"

She couldn't, or wouldn't, finish her sentence. Tyrone looked at the floor again. There were a few metal shavings right next to a few…cookie crumbs? "Frank. Look at this."

Frank bent down and examined the floor. He picked up a crumb and put it to his lips. "Oatmeal Chocolate Chip. Oh my God."

Tyrone straightened and looked right at Liv. "Like a whole family of cookie cutters?"

Liv's eyes widened and she nodded vigorously.

Meanwhile, the house around them filled with strange noises. Clicks and creaks, squeaks and rustling. They could hear the noises, but didn't pay any attention.

Frank asked, "How did you find them?"

"How did you know what they were?" Jeremy asked. The other three looked at him, surprised. This was the first time he'd spoken since they had reunited.

"Our question first, Jeremy," Tyrone said.

"No," Jeremy replied. Their leader looked grim. He would not debate. "You two know more about it than we do. How did we get stuck in a house with living cookie cutters?"

Tyrone stepped forward. "I found them in a box downstairs. Frank helped me open it. I thought there might be something valuable inside. Frank, though, he found the…incantation in another room. We didn't even know they went together, but after I read it, the cookie cutters disappeared and next thing we heard was Liv here screaming her head off," Tyrone explained. "So, why were you screaming?"

"One of them was on me. On my back. Jeremy said he thought it was a rat. It wasn't."

"Can I see?" Frank asked. Liv stayed still for a moment, then half turned and pulled her shirt up. A small current of blood was running down her back, and there was an imprint near her left shoulder blade.

The outline of a small gingerbread boy.

"Oh God. Oh God. We've got to call the police! Oh G—"

"Shut up, Liv," Jeremy cut in. "We can't call the cops. What do you think we're doing here? We are criminals. Unless you can add to the collective intelligence in the room, just shut up."

She complied, but sat as far away from him as possible. Jeremy had buttoned his shirt and folded his arms across his chest. Liv, on the other hand, was still holding her bra, and her shoes were on the floor by the bed.

Tyrone squinted at Jeremy. "You might be right about the cops, but being a jerk isn't going to help anything right now."

"You got all the answers, T? Is having your ex-girlfriend on speed dial going to solve everything for us? In a haunted house? Besides, I've seen this movie before and you'll be the first to go."

Tyrone opened his mouth to let Jeremy have it, but shut it again. It wouldn't have mattered. Frank took over.

"Both of you, shut it. We've got a problem. Yes, Tyrone and I started it, but we didn't know we were doing it. Instead of sniping at each other, we need to get out of here. Liv's shoulder means that those damn cookie cutters are a-okay with drawing blood. And if it's true that Jeremy stomped on Junior, a little cut is probably not what we should expect from here on out," Frank stated.

The room fell silent. Tyrone felt the mantle of leadership shift from Jeremy to Frank. Jeremy wouldn't like it, but Frank was showing who could and probably would get them home alive. Frank looked around and craned his head out of the room briefly.

"Okay. So we'll head down the stairs together. I don't see any problems right now. Maybe it's all over."

Tyrone felt something crawl over his shoe. Instinctively, he jumped about three feet in the air. "What the..." He swung his flashlight around the floor, catching a flash of silver by the doorframe as whatever it was ran out of the room.

Jeremy hopped off the bed, looking around wildly. "Forget your stupid plan, Frank. Time to go!" He was out the door before anyone could even raise an objection. Their once-fearless leader was first down the upstairs hallway, leaving poor Liv behind with Frank and Tyrone. A few seconds later, they heard a few thuds from the direction of the staircase, but Tyrone attributed it to Jeremy's eagerness to get the heck out of Dodge.

Tyrone saw a panicked expression on Liv's face. "I guess I know how he really feels about me. Will you guys keep me safe?"

"You got it, Liv," Tyrone said. "Frank, you leading the way? I'll bring up the rear. Let's go. I bet Jeremy's already curled up in a ball in the back of the van."

Frank laughed and stepped into the hall. The house was quiet. Too quiet. Tyrone silently cursed Jeremy. He probably was already in the van, possibly even speeding away, leaving them behind. Jerk.

They reached the steep staircase and looked down. Tyrone revised his opinion. A dead jerk.

Somewhere in the back of his mind, Tyrone could hear Liv's screams, but for a few seconds, the world went quiet. Part of him wanted to believe that Jeremy was faking it. That he was still alive, but the blood...the blood loss was...

Jeremy was dead. And if they were going to get out of the house, someone was going to have to move his body.

He was twisted in a mangled heap at the base of the stairwell, kitchen knives jutting out of nearly every part of his body.

"T? You with us, man?"

Tyrone looked over and noticed Frank holding onto Liv so tightly, it looked like he thought if he let go, she would immediately fly into a million little pieces.

"Yeah, I'm here."

Liv peeked around Frank. "Wha—what happened?"

Tyrone crouched down and looked down at the first step. It looked...greasy. He ran his finger through it, then smelled it.

"Crisco."

"What?" Frank asked.

"The little devils coated the step with Crisco," he repeated. His eyes traced the steps down to the floor where Jeremy's body was crumpled. "If I had to guess, I'd say Jeremy hit this step going about sixty miles an hour, went flying, and landed on whatever trap the cookie cutters had waiting for him at the bottom."

He paused, nearly retching. He'd been in the hospital room with his grandfather when he passed away a couple years ago, but a silent heart monitor was vastly different from seeing a human voodoo doll jammed with a dozen knives.

"I don't trust those stairs," Frank said. "We don't know what else they might have at the bottom, especially since we'll have to get past Jeremy's body."

"He's a mess. I don't know—" Tyrone said.

Frank interrupted, "He's already dead. We can't—"

"Stop saying that!" Liv screeched.

Tyrone and Frank stopped talking.

Frank gripped Liv's shoulders and held her so she could see his face. "Liv, I wasn't always a fan of Jeremy's.

T knows that and he'd say the same thing. Did either of us want him dead? Absolutely not. But right now we don't have the luxury of calling a funeral home and getting emotional. We can mourn him later. First, we need to survive. Okay?"

She sniffed, then nodded.

"What's next, Frank?" Tyrone asked.

Frank's hulking form seemed to freeze for a second. He looked down the stairs, then back down the hallway they'd just come from.

"Well, I still think going downstairs is dumb. Maybe we shouldn't be on the second floor, but maybe there's an easy drop from a window. If nothing else, we'll do the old Hollywood trick of tying bedsheets together. What do you think?"

Tyrone considered the plan for a second. "Yeah. Let's see what's up here. Liv, you were already up here when Frank and I ran up the stairs. Thoughts?"

It was clear that Liv was going to do whatever Frank said at this point, but Tyrone wanted her to be actively engaged in their escape.

"Yeah. Let's go."

Frank led the way, with Liv behind him and Tyrone in the rear. The old house creaked and moaned, but Tyrone didn't know what was normal and what was part of the curse they'd inadvertently brought upon themselves. He flinched at every slight noise. From the end of the hall, he could see five doors, three on the left and two on the right.

On the right, the first one was the bedroom where Liv and Jeremy were...busy, when he first came up. Frank reached the first door on the left and tried the knob. Locked.

"We'll come back if we need to, but let's see what the other rooms are. Good?"

Tyrone and Liv were both out of words, instead just nodding.

They moved on to the next door on the left. Frank struggled with the latch, but finally pushed it open, revealing a small staircase leading up. An attic. Up wasn't the direction they were looking for. They kept going.

At the last two doors, directly across from each other, Frank positioned himself by the one on the right and Tyrone moved to the other door. Liv took a step back.

"Let's open them at the same time and get this over with," Tyrone said.

"Fine with me," Frank replied.

As they moved to open the doors, Liv asked, "Do you smell something burning?"

Frank had already opened his door, a plume of smoke now snaking out of the bedroom. Tyrone had his own room open, but his attention was on Frank, who was eerily silent.

"Frank?"

Tyrone pushed past Liv and peered into Frank's room. Just inside the door he saw an ironing board with a red-hot iron on its side. It was hard to see, but next to it stood a four-inch tall metal woman, what he thought of as mom. The outline of a mother cookie cutter, at least. Tyrone grabbed Frank's arm to pull him away, but noticed the only thing keeping Frank upright was the doorframe. Just below his chin was a thin line of blood. A flash of silver near his neck made Tyrone jump back.

"What is it?" Liv asked, her voice low and surprisingly calm.

"I...I don't know," Tyrone answered, but he thought he might.

He looked back at the ironing board. Mom had moved slightly, standing now in front of the red-hot iron. Tyrone knew he had to move quickly. He shoved Frank's shoulder to get a look at him. He had two wounds. The smaller one was in his chest, but it was still sizeable—about as big as a girl-shaped cookie cutter. Two inches is huge when you're talking about a puncture wound. The other went right into his neck. The "Dad" cutter was still embedded in Frank's neck, severing his throat and esophagus.

"Oh my god. He's dead." Liv said it like a casual comment. Not a question. Not even ten minutes past Jeremy's death and now it was already commonplace for the girl.

From what Tyrone could tell, it looked like the cutters superheated themselves and jumped Frank when he opened the door, killing him almost instantly and simultaneously cauterizing the wounds. Frank's eyes showed a hint of life, and then in an instant he was gone, his body collapsing onto the hardwood floor. Another quick look at Mom told Tyrone he needed to move. He turned and shoved Liv into the bedroom he'd just opened and slammed the door closed behind them.

Liv seemed nonplussed, and said, "We're all going to die," like it was routine.

Tyrone grabbed her shoulders and stared into her eyes. Eyes that had nearly checked out. Nearly.

"Not if I can help it. Stay with me, Liv. These are just a couple of metal cookie cutters. They aren't going to beat us."

"They beat Jeremy. And Frank. Oh, poor Frank…" Liv replied, her eyes watering. She seemed to be taking Frank's death harder than Jeremy's. She sniffed. "I'll be next, and then you."

"Maybe. I won't deny it's likely, but we know what we're facing. Jeremy was stupid, and Frank... well Frank should still be here. If anyone should have been next, it should have been me."

Liv deadpanned, "You aren't being very helpful."

"I know. I know. Frank's idea wasn't bad, though. Let's see what's out the windows in here."

There was just one window, directly opposite the door. The latch caught for a few seconds from the rust of decades of inattention, but Tyrone's determination won out. He pushed the fragile frame open. There was barely any light, so Tyrone turned on his flashlight and looked down at the ground. Most of it was clear. There was grass under the window. An oak tree stood about fifteen feet away; a couple of its branches nearly touched the house.

Liv backed away from the window. "I can't, Tyrone."

"What do you mean? This is the way out. We can leave right now."

"I—what if I fall? I don't think I can. Let's go back. Let's try the stairs."

Tyrone shook his head. "We can't do that. You saw what happened to Jeremy. Who knows what else is down there?"

"But..."

"This is it. Our best chance. Look, I'll go first, and then you follow me. I'm heading for that branch right there. It's sturdy enough. We get on it and then we can climb down to the ground. See? The van is right over there."

She considered his words for a moment. "Fine. Go. I'll follow you."

It'd been at least a decade and a half since Tyrone had climbed a tree, and never with so much on the line. He stepped out of the window onto a small ledge underneath that let him scoot over to the branch. He tested it for a few seconds then shuffled as quickly as he could to the branch, then over to the trunk. He looked for Liv, and saw she was behind him. If the branch held him, it should be able to hold three of her, no problem. He held his breath anyway, and his heart nearly stopped a few times before she reached him.

"You made it."

"Did you think I wouldn't?" Liv asked.

"After seeing what happened to Frank, I have no expectations."

"Fair enough. Let's get out of here."

They picked their way down the old tree and ran to the van.

Tyrone slowed as he got closer. "Wait. What about the keys?"

She pulled something from her pocket and jangled them in the air. For a brief moment, the flash of the metal reminded Tyrone of the cookie cutters, but the familiar sound of keys brought him back to reality. "Jeremy hated having stuff in his pockets. He made me carry them."

"Great. Why don't you go ahead and start it up? I'm going to make a quick phone call."

"Meg?"

"Yeah…"

She smiled. "Go ahead, T. I think we've got a few seconds."

She clambered into the driver's seat and the next thing Tyrone heard was the door shutting and the ignition turning over. He dug the phone out of his pocket and pressed the numbers he knew by heart. Once again, the call went to voicemail. Once again, he didn't pass up a chance to leave a message. He turned away from the van.

"Meg. It's Tyrone again. Duh. Well, I just wanted to hear your voice, but I guess I can wait a bit longer. I uh—I had an experience tonight. I thought I was going to die, but, obviously I didn't. Anyway, whatever happened between us, it was all my fault. I'm sorry for everything. I just want to be with you. Even if things suck sometimes and we can't buy bread, I just want to be with you. I just want—"

He was interrupted by a cut off scream.

Liv.

Tyrone slowly turned back toward the van. He didn't need confirmation to know Liv was already gone. Dammit. She'd trusted him and where had it led her? He shined his flashlight into the cab and saw blood smeared all over the windows, but a clear spot revealed a silvery man atop the steering wheel. He heard a click and realized there was more than one. Mom, Dad, and Little Girl were all working together, because the next thing he knew the van lurched at him. One of them was pressing on the gas pedal. He didn't know how, but he knew the dad was staring him down. One last human on his cookie cutter list of vengeance.

He turned and ran, then realized he was still on Meg's voicemail.

"Yeah. So...yeah. That whole 'almost died' thing, I guess isn't quite over. Turns out Frank and I accidentally awakened a set of cursed cookie cutters. They're currently trying to kill me, so if you don't hear from me again, that's what happened. I'm going to stop talking now. Love you!"

He tried to end the call, but wasn't sure if he did or not. Then he stopped worrying about the status of his phone call. He ran back to the house. If all the cutters were in the van, then the house should be relatively safe.

A thought crossed his mind. The incantation. The sampler. The one Frank had found and brought to him. The stupid thing that had started it all. Maybe, if there was one that brought the insane things to life, there was one that would put them back to sleep. He had nothing to lose. He shot through the unlocked front door, looking for the sewing room. He passed the kitchen on his right and saw a room to the left with fabric from floor to ceiling. He went in and slammed the door, knowing perfectly well if the murderous family of cookie cutters wanted in, there probably wasn't a darn thing he could do to stop them.

Using his flashlight as his guide, he toured the room, focusing a second on each handmade sampler. Tyrone saw more than a few alphabets and a couple of The Lord's Prayer, but nothing that reminded him of the incantation he'd read earlier that had breathed life into the small metal people. What if…

His train of thought was interrupted by what he could have sworn was a train crashing into the house. The van. The cookie cutters must have built up enough speed to make a decent impact and hit the house. For whatever reason, it brought back a memory less than an hour old of Frank smashing the locked box in the kitchen. The kitchen…

That's where they'd brought them to life. That's where the box had been smashed. That's where they'd left the two-verse poem. The poem in a frame…

A thought nagged him. He might die, but he had to check it out.

Tyrone dashed out of the sewing room—pausing briefly to see the damage by the front door where Jeremy's van rested— and zoomed towards the kitchen.

A metallic clink pinged a few inches from his right ear, but he didn't have time to stop. He plunged ahead, catching sight of the framed stitching on the kitchen table. Tyrone picked it up and flipped it over.

Nothing.

Something flicked his left ear. He instinctively ducked and grabbed his earlobe. He saw bright red blood. They had a taste for him. He was a goner.

In a fit of rage, Tyrone threw the incantation against the fridge. The glass shattered and the fabric tumbled out of the wooden frame. Picking it up, he saw another verse to the poem, tucked below what he'd innocently read aloud earlier.

He felt a slash at his abdomen. Another at his ankle. He danced as if it was simply a few mosquitos he was battling instead of a few psychotic cookie cutters. He tried to shine his light on the fabric, and began to read. As he did, the three remaining family members sliced at his legs and arms, but Tyrone pushed on.

When again They need to sleep
Lay their heads and count their sheep
Gather them all. Enchantment be gone!
Safe and secure in their home once again

As soon as the last word emerged from Tyrone's lips, the three cookie cutters clattered to the aged vinyl floor. He pointed the flashlight in their direction and saw blood splashed and splattered everywhere around the cookie cutters. They were covered in blood, but after Frank and Liv, Tyrone couldn't be sure it was all his. He felt sick to his stomach, but didn't run right away. The lockbox had been broken, so that was out. Tyrone didn't want to smash the cookie cutters. He doubted the police would believe him, but part of him wanted to preserve the evidence, regardless. After kicking them around the kitchen a while, he picked them up and threw them into the refrigerator, then found some duct tape to keep the door shut.

Just in case.

He walked towards the front of the house. He couldn't even bring himself to look at the van or what was left of Liv, but picked a path away from the century-old dwelling.

Even with the threat contained, Tyrone nearly jumped a mile high when his phone rang, blaring an electronic chime in his ear. He dug the phone out and saw the Caller ID. He smiled.

"Meg, I can't tell you how great it is to hear your voice…"

Tyrone scratched his shoulder as he talked, wishing whatever bug crawling inside his shirt would leave him alone.

Third Shift
Terry R. Hill

"DR. ABERCROMBIE, YOU MISSED missed the Christmas party!"

Dr. Richard Abercrombie looked up from the patient clipboard toward the sickly-sweet voice reeking of virgin punch and homemade fudge. Nurse Cynthia Adams stood beaming before him, full of holiday cheer and crowned with blinking red-foam antlers.

"Sorry, I wasn't in the mood for Whoville," he mumbled. For a brief moment, confusion crossed her face. But just as quickly, she shrugged her shoulders and continued on with her mission of contaminating others with cheer.

At thirty-eight this was where his promising medical career had landed him: as a general practitioner in a mid-sized, forgettable hospital in the middle of Missouri. Not where he'd envisioned himself winding up, and a fact that his father never missed an opportunity to remind him of.

'If you'd learned to play the system rather than fight it, you'd have gone further, but instead you burned too many bridges along the way, and with each one, you closed a door.'

Old men were expert Monday-morning quarterbacks for the young.

The whole Christmas thing, he wasn't feeling it. And here he was covering the shifts of two doctors so they could be with their young families over the holidays. Yeah, he could have said no, but it wasn't like he was going to spend it with his dad or even his wife…anymore.

Wha…what? Uggg.

A few seconds of confused grogginess later, he located the source of the noise. The thirty-minute alarm he'd set was going off. Being yanked out of deep sleep was never pleasant, but such was the life of a doctor.

Ugg. Day three of continuous shifts. Hmm. Christmas Eve. Merry freaking Christmas, guys.

But there were still patients to see, reports to review, and paperwork to sign-off. He'd only seen his wife's requests through the window of a holiday he didn't believe in. As it turned out, they were her last attempts to reach out and reconnect with her absent husband. If only hindsight wasn't so damned obvious. With some effort, he stood, slowly, all the while his back and knees protested.

This must be what seventy-five feels like, and why geriatric patients complain all the time.

Running his fingers through his thinning hair caused some mild discomfort. He got the same response when he rubbed his arms in an effort to shake the chill of the darkened staff nap room. Not good. For him, those were the unmistakable signs of the flu.

"How lucky am I?" he mumbled. The one year he didn't get the flu shot.

Life, you're being a real bitch. You know that, right?

The bright light of the hospital corridor shot through his eyes with force as he emerged from the nap room. Slowly, the brightness became tolerable as he stumbled to the break room to see if there was any coffee left. This time of the morning, it was generally thick enough to scrape across some toast.

Great. Not even any sludge.

Richard shuffled to the nearest nurses' station, the friction of his scrubs against the skin of his legs was almost painful. Better get control of the symptoms before they get hold of him if he was going to cover everyone's shifts. For God's sake, he was a doctor; the virus was no match for him and twenty-first century medicine.

"Sarah, I need a couple of vitamin C, some Tylenol, and a 24hr. Claritin," he said to the nurse behind the desk. She disappeared into the small room behind her station and re-emerged a few moments later.

"Here you go, Honey. Not feeling good?"

He threw the pills down this throat.

"Feeling great. Oh, and the coffee needs to be made."

Sarah's mood visibly changed. Placing her hand on her ample hip and cocking an eyebrow, she said, "Excuse me? I ain't your mamma! Make your own damn coffee."

He stared at her for a minute. She could easily take him if she was inclined to do so. Probably not worth it for 2 a.m. coffee.

"Fine," he mumbled while leaving.

Did the hospital administration really expect the doctors, who spent almost two decades of their lives learning how to fix the incredibly complex human machine, to now spend their very valuable time each day making freaking coffee? Really? Wasn't that something someone who got paid less per hour normally did? Was that so unreasonable to expect? To keep your over-worked doctors somewhat mentally coherent? Okay, maybe not the nurses, but at least the people working the front desk could swing by once an hour to make sure the coffee flowed freely. Yeah, he'd probably been a bit snippy to Sarah. He should go back and smooth things over with her. It would likely cost him if he didn't; Sarah could be a tough cookie.

"Yes?" Sarah asked with an air of expectancy when he returned to the nurses' station fifteen minutes later.

"I…uh. Look, sorry I was short with you earlier. I'm just a bit tired."

She smiled. "Now that's better. Here's your coffee, Hun. Now, was that so hard?" she said, handing him a cup of fresh steaming coffee. It even had creamer the way he liked it.

"Thank…you. How did you know—"

"You're not the only observant one around here. Merry Christmas, Sugar. Now go play doctor for a few more hours, and then get some rest. Nurse's orders."

All he could do was smile. It had been a long time. It felt good.

"Dr. Abercrombie, please report to the ER immediately," squawked the hospital intercom.

Great. The early morning lull didn't last long. It would be interesting to see what creative, self-inflicted injury the never-ending stream of local bubbas, who kept the ER busy, had come up with this morning. Would it be shotgun roulette, or kitchen-knife chicken, or beer can off the head William Tell style? The options with these guys were limitless.

As he pushed through the ER doors, a frantic scene greeted him: the ambulance paramedics, along with most of the emergency room nurses, were struggling to hold down a man screaming as if he were possessed by Satan himself.

"What did you bring me this time, Dave?" Richard asked. Dave Sweet, one of the paramedics with whom he'd developed a work friendship, had patched together more nightmares on the battle field during his military days than Richard had ever seen on the operating table. So the two shared stories when things were a little slow.

"Hey, Doc." Dave grunted while restraining an arm and shoulder of the raging man on the stretcher, "We have an approximately thirty- to forty-year-old male, unknown medical history, medications, or allergies. Patient was non-verbal but responsive to painful stimuli. Visible trauma to the left calf, probable animal bite. IV access established en route, 18 gauge in the right AC. Vital signs: BP 165 over 96, HR 140, sinus tachycardia, no ectopic beats. Blood glucose 122. Respiratory rate 26, shallow, SpO2 93, O2 administered via Non-Rebreather at 15 lpm. Patient become agitated about fifteen minutes out. I hit him with 5 mg of Haldol and 2.5 mg of Midazolam about ten minutes before arrival...no affect. Once we rolled into ER, vitals went haywire. Heart rate began to climb, and pressure started dropping."

"Where did you find him?" asked Richard.

"Found supine on the ground out in the woods by hunters out on Old US 63, over by the animal research facility."

"In the middle of the woods in the middle of the night, huh? Probably not spot-lighting deer for Christmas dinner, huh?" said Richard.

"Yeah, probably not," replied Cassie with a strained smirk and trying her best to hold onto the struggling man's feet. Cassie was Dave's partner and, on more than one occasion, he'd mentioned she was probably smarter than most of the medics he'd known, Richard being an exception of course.

"Get some leathers on this guy," Richard barked at the nurse not holding onto the victim.

"That's what I'm trying to do," she replied, annoyance clear in her voice as she readied the restraints.

Somehow the patient freed his arms, sat up, and began clawing at his own face, tearing the flesh from the bone as if it were on fire.

Frantic arms grasped his in an effort to stop the unfolding horror.

Still sitting, though with his arms immobilized once again, the patient violently shook his bloody head, splattering all those in the room with chunks of himself and his bodily fluids.

"Restraints, dammit. One up, one down! Left arm by his head!" Richard bellowed.

"Done," reported a nurse a few seconds later. Now with many practiced hands in motion, the patient's legs were next.

"His IV's out. Dave, help me hold his arm still. Nurse give him 10 mg of Haldol IM to help him chill out," ordered Richard.

This should put a smile on his face.

A few minutes passed. No effect. John Doe still jerked his limbs, frantically battling the restraints.

Richard scanned the room. All the nurses were looking to him for direction. Dave's eyebrow was cocked in question.

"Okay. Give him 6 mg of Adenosine and 10 mg of Versed."

Moments later, a nurse administered the second shot. The amount of sedative should have been enough knock out a four-hundred-pound man. This man was a couple hundred pounds shy of the mark. Four, three, two, one…

Still no results. The patient thrashed against the straps as if nothing had happened, and the vital monitors beeped like frenetic metronomes.

"Doctor, he's at 175 b.p.m. and climbing. Doctor, he's going unstable."

Shit. What's going on inside this man? Has he been smoking bath salts or something? He was even beginning to exhibit frothy spittle.

John Doe jumped and stiffened as if an electrical pulse ran through him.

A constant, unwavering tone issued from the heart rate monitor, but there was no recovery.

"He's gone asystolic," reported a nurse.

Shit!

"Get an IV in and give him some epinephrine!" Richard barked. The soft thud of the beginnings of CPR onto John Doe's chest followed.

Tone…bleep, bleep.

An audible sigh of relief escaped Richard's lips.

The patience's heart rate returned to normal, and he slowly began to relax, staring blindly into space. Within a moment or two, the patient almost seemed peaceful. Alive, although unresponsive.

The monitor beeped in the background with a comforting, slow rhythm.

"Wow. Can you guys manage not to bring any more like him in today?" Richard asked jokingly. Laughter bubbled across the room, everyone needing a little release from the last half hour. The smiling faces surrounding him looked as if they had all stood too close to an industrial strength strawberry smoothie blender and not used a lid. What a mess.

The patient moved his lips and quietly whimpered, drawing the attention of the room.

The man locked into a rigor, almost hovering above the sheets of the stretcher, and let loose with a scream from hell itself before crashing again. The cardiac monitor toned flat.

"Holy shit," Richard heard someone say. Maybe it was himself.

Frantic moments of attempted resuscitation passed in a heartbeat.

A cold chill ran down his back. He never got used to losing patients. Every time he did, it sucked just like this. However, this time he could be in for additional headaches due to that last shot of meds.

Ah! Of course.

"Dave, did you say he'd been attacked by an animal?"

"Yes."

"Hmm. The crazed aggression… It's all pointing to rabies. Run a brain tissue sample under the scope to confirm," Richard ordered.

"Doctor?" asked one of the nurses.

Cassie knowingly nudged Dave.

"Doc, it's only been about three hours ago that the attack was reported. Unless someone is bitten by a rabid animal very close to the spinal column near the brain stem, which he wasn't, it takes days to weeks for it to advance to this stage in humans."

"Then let's hope it's not rabies."

Bzzzzz, Bzzzzz ... Bzzzz, Bzzzz ... Bzzzz, Bzzzz

"What? What do you want?" Richard groaned as he sat up on the bed in the sleep room and picked up his buzzing phone with a few waiting text messages.

What time is it? 5 a.m.? He'd intended to only catch a few minutes of sleep, but it had been almost two hours. Evidently, he'd forgotten to set his alarm and the nurses must have been feeling kind and let him sleep. What did they want anyway? God his head hurt. Felt like those headaches from undergrad days the morning after you really tied one on.

<Report to ER. Mass Casualty Event. Traffic pile-up.>

<Numerous casualties expected.>

Great.

Richard shuffled to the washroom and turned on the small light. Jesus, he looked rough. Almost as bad as he felt.

Note to self: Don't ever take two other people's shifts in addition to your own at the same time.

...and he still had on the bloodied scrubs from the dead guy. Nice.

Within a few moments, he'd washed his face, changed into a clean pair of scrubs, and...he felt worse than ever.

"Hey, Dick," said Dr. Shultz, the only other doctor on duty, and one who should have retired a decade ago.

"Richard."

"Right. Anyway, I didn't see you and Susan at Dr. Petterson's party."

Richard took a deep breath. Explaining the way things were now had become tedious, and dealing with people's emotional reactions even more bothersome.

"Susan and I separated in the spring," he replied.

"Ah. The plight of the doctor. My first three wives did the same thing. You're young. You can still saddle up a few more times before you get my age. Just remember the pre-nup next time. The first one is always the most expensive," he said as he turned and wandered toward ICU. Not exactly the expected response, but admittedly when a man had lived as long as Shultz had, death probably didn't impress him much either.

"Yeah. Thanks," he replied to Shultz.

Do a nice thing by covering other's shifts and I'm rewarded by being trapped here with Old Man Captain Obvious.

"Sarah, I need more vitamin C and Tylenol. No, make that a double," he said as he passed the nurses station before launching into a series of sneezes.

"And Claritin."

"Okay, but don't you go sneezing all over my desk. Keep your damn germs to yourself!" she replied.

With a wink and a quick toast, he slammed back the pills and made his way to the ER.

"What do we have coming in?" Richard asked one of the ER nurses who was busily prepping the different stations about the room.

"There is a report of a twenty-car pile-up on Interstate 70 due to icy roads and a dense fog that rolled in unexpectedly. Ambulances from around the five-county area are being called in. We're the biggest hospital around, so expect dozens of injured and dead. My guess is they'll start arriving here any moment. Paramedics have handed out tags and first story is that we have five red, ten yellow, eleven green, and four black," he replied, focused on getting things ready for the next wave.

"Damn," Richard said under his breath. "Families on the road for Christmas."

"Yep," said the nurse.

A small stream of watery snot ran down Richard's face, which he wiped away with some annoyance.

The meds needed to kick in soon. Can't deal with my own symptoms and patients at the same time.

He ran toward the nurses' station. They needed to call in all the doctors available.

Sorry, John and Chris, we're calling you in.

They wouldn't get in 'til well after the first wave of patients, but better late than never. With all hands on deck, there would be no way for him to leave once they arrived anyway, due to the sheer number of incoming casualties and all of the follow-up required.

"Sarah. Call in all the docs."

"Already done, Hun. You know this place wouldn't operate without me, right?"

Richard snickered. Sadly, there was probably more truth to her words than he'd like.

"All doctors to the ER. Patients arriving. All doctors to the ER," echoed through the halls of the hospital mostly empty of the normal number of doctors.

Damnit, they're here.

The only way he and Shultz could manage until the others got in was to save the ones they could, and let the less serious cases wait.

The doors burst open and stretchers and paramedics streamed in.

"What do you have?" Richard called out.

"Eight- to ten-year-old female, head trauma, multiple lacerations and broken collar bone. Patient is unconscious and IV access established en route. Vital signs: blood glucose normal. Respiratory is shallow, and blood pressure is dropping."

Crap. A kid.

Severely injured kids always got to Richard. Thank God he didn't have any, he'd be a constant nervous wreck.

"I got this one," said Shultz from behind. Shultz wasn't his favorite person in the world, but the man wasn't afraid of stepping up when it mattered.

Seconds later, Dave and Cassie showed up with a middle-aged man with multiple tibia and fibula open fractures, a C-spine injury, and early signs of hypothermia. Evidently the fire crew had to use jaws of life on this one. The patient would be touch and go, but would probably survive.

The stream of critically to moderately injured continued for some time and would eventually end with the arrival of the dead. The human body just was not designed to take the impact loads of two-ton vehicles screaming down the road four to six times the fastest speed humans were designed to run. Skull and facial fractures, lacerations of all sorts, broken bones, amputations, you name it, they all came in. But his job was to stabilize the patient in front of him then move to the next. Looking down the long list of patients waiting and their conditions was like a high-rise steel worker looking down and seeing how small the cars were down below. Not helpful.

His head felt like it was caught in an invisible vice, threatening to split open at any moment. Watering eyes and a streaming nose made him resort to shoving ear plugs into his nostrils to stop the running long enough to work over a patient. But with the near incessant sneezing, the plugs didn't stay long. One sneeze caught Richard off guard. The plugs dislodged, and flew across the exam room. Admittedly, it was pretty damn funny.

In between patients, he popped more pills ranging from over the counter could remedies to pain medications to mild stimulants. The additional doctors had made it in, but he had to keep pushing too.

On his way past an empty exam station in the receiving room, a swarm of sneezes attacked. When he'd recovered, it was clear he'd sprayed a container of tongue depressors. Gross. He'd let a nurse know and have them replaced.

"Dr. Abercrombie, another ambulance has arrived and everyone else is busy. Can you attend?" a nurse asked as he ran past toward the receiving door.

It was a mother and young son. Not too bad. Just need to check both of them for possible injuries. He put on a face mask to hide the red mess his nose had become and to catch any sneeze he couldn't stifle.

Things were going well until a sneeze, originating from somewhere in his toes, caught him off guard and blew a hole clear through his mask, covering the mother and son.

"Oh…God. I'm so sorry," he exclaimed. The two sat shocked at their new, wet situation.

"I…I've never had that happen before. Please forgive me." This was no good. If he couldn't control things better than this, he was of no use to the patients.

"Hun, how many hours have you been on duty?" Sarah asked as he stood in the hallway, contemplating what to do.

"Huh? Oh. I don't know. Two days, three? Hard to keep track."

"Go home, Richard. We appreciate you pulling all these hours, but we're all in now," said Dr. John Wagner who'd overheard Richard's reply.

"Thanks, John, but there's still too much follow up over the next shift for just you guys. I'm going to go to my office and catch an hour or so nap."

"Richard, just—" said John.

"Seriously, I'm okay. Just need a little rest," replied Richard.

Just because he's fresh doesn't mean he has any right to tell me what I can and can't do. Damn young'uns.

With the blackout blinds drawn, the office was dark and relatively quiet. Richard pushed all of the trade magazines, books and random bits of clothing off of his couch and wadded up the sports jacket he'd taken off the back of his desk chair for a pillow. Even under the best of circumstances, his body would hurt like it was on the edge of revolt after a third shift, much less a third day. Add on a case of the flu and, yeah, it was pretty much unbearable. Soon, there would be sleep. A short nap and he'd be good until the end of the day. Then he could take some time off, recover, and miss all of the retelling of their cute Christmas stories and how adorable the kids were on Christmas morning, and how the guys all got lucky that night when the jewelry was found underneath the tree. Yeah, no need to be around for all of that.

There was something unsettling about Crazy John Doe this morning. What a bizarre case. What could it have been? The symptoms and timeline of probable infection vector just didn't line up. There was something hanging on the edge of his mind; some clue, some data that was important but was being held back for some reason. Maybe it was because his freaking head felt like it was going to explode! Or because his heart was beating like he just ran up the stairs! Who could sleep with that?

Hands shaking, he got off the couch and began rummaging through one of the desk drawers. It was where all the samples the shameless drug reps filled his hands with at least once a week ended up. Packet after packet, he ripped them open. Various pain pills and beta-blockers piled up on the desk.

That should do it, he thought before shoveling the assortment into his mouth and washing them down with a bottle of water.

God, that tastes awful. Wonder how long that's been on the desk?

Maybe doing some paperwork would numb his mind enough to help him fall asleep. Or at least keep him occupied until the meds kicked in and offered some relief. He signed into his computer and a backlog of 'paperwork' greeted him. This ought to keep me busy for a while.

Richard skimmed a few of the online forms regarding patients from the day before. The previous twenty-four hours were nothing like the last few. So many wounded in such a short time. It was just unheard of for their neck of the country.

A sneezing fit grabbed hold of him and didn't relinquish control of his body until every muscle between his shoulders and his groin were spasming and screaming at him. He fell to the floor and forced himself into a position something like a backward yoga pose to help release the cramps. Plus, all the sneezing forced a lot of blood up into his head, which now pounded like a jackhammer.

Shit, it hurts.

When the last abdominal muscle relaxed, he slowly crawled back up into the desk chair. Oh gross. He'd coated his monitor with the contents of his sinuses.

John Doe. There was just something about that man which didn't sit well. There had been plenty of drugged-out nut jobs fighting against god-knows-what in their minds when they came into the ER over the years, but this guy was different. He was in a completely different place than the others. Doe wasn't lashing out at a hallucination, he was trying to rip himself and everyone else to shreds. His eyes were clear and focused, small pupils. Not dilated or with a vacant stare. Every action was deliberate.

The more he thought about it, the more the rabies pathology made sense. But the timeline was all off from the time and location of exposure, to the onset of symptoms. Something else had to be at play. Hell, they had given Doe enough Haldol, Adenosine, and Versed to knock out a two-ton bull. But it would be sometime before the labs were back in. If it was rabies, then there was no way they would have been able to save Doe anyway once the symptoms manifested to that level.

A sudden wave of intolerable irritation swept over him. Aahhh! What's the point of all of this crap anyway?

The only thing he'd accomplished was wasting more of his life and talents in this go-nowhere hospital, patching up Darwin Award candidates with even more pointless lives. It would actually be doing them a tremendous favor if he helped them all along to the other side to be in their even more pathetic afterlife. A loud snap of a plastic pen shattering in his hand broke him from his thoughts.

Whoa! Where did that come from?

Shards of the pen in one hand and a small stack of scrunched papers in the other. If he didn't chill out, he wouldn't be in any shape to help downstairs later. But where did those thoughts come from? Did he really believe those things, somewhere far beneath the surface?

By the time he'd finished all the damn paperwork, it was well after 8 a.m., Christmas freaking Day. Ho Freaking Ho. He hadn't slept a wink, either. The attempted work-induced sleep-aid had failed him.

There was no denying it, he was feeling pretty crappy. No, make that incredibly shitty. More specifically, like death warmed over. His lungs were raw with the non-stop coughing, runny nose glowed with soreness, and the damn sneezing had gotten so bad it was a wonder he hadn't found his eyeballs sitting on his desk staring back at him. Yes, he had a full-blown case of the goddamned flu on Christmas.

Ahhh! Damn it!

He slammed his fist onto his desk, causing everything on it to shake and pain to lance up his arm.

Calm down, Richard. Breathe.

But there was an undeniable sense of frustration, irritation bubbling below the surface. Maybe it was just pent up stress after working so many shifts. Maybe because of the wonderful place his life had ended up with one failed relationship—personal or otherwise.

A chuckle escaped his sore chest. Who was he trying to kid? This was likely just the true ego of Dr. Richard Martin Abercrombie, the true unadulterated asshole, finally coming out now that he no longer gave a royal shit about anything.

Either way, he was a sick asshole who needed to take his war with the flu to the next level. Retrieving a sterilized sample collection kit from the cabinet behind the desk, he collected oral and nasal samples and sealed the containers. Poking his head outside his office, he flagged down a passing nurse.

"Run these to the lab and have them tested and cultured immediately. Tell them to let me know what they find out right away."

"Yes, doctor. If I may say so, you look terrible. You should get some rest or go home," offered the nurse.

"Is that..." Richard stopped himself, jaw clenching. Something popped. Unclear if it was his jaw or a filling. Damn it. Just what I need—medical advice from the nurses. "Thank you, Nurse."

His phone started buzzing. It was the ER.

"Yes?"

"Dr. Abercrombie, one of the traffic accident patients is crashing, we need you in the ER."

Moments later, Richard rushed into room. It was still filled with those who were badly injured and had not yet been moved to ICU or private rooms. After receiving a quick set of vitals from the attending nurse, he said, "Give him six milligrams of Adenosine to get his heart rate down."

"We did. It's not working," said the nurse moments later.

Monitors began toning with a flat line. Movement erupted in the room.

"Get the pads ready. Go!" Richard barked.

The man's body jumped. Nothing.

"Again."

Nothing.

"Again."

Nothing. Damn.

"Okay. Time of death, 10:32 a.m." said Richard.

His phone buzzed again. Who was it this time? It was a hospital number.

"Yes?"

"Is this Dr. Abercrombie?"

"Yes."

"This is Dr. Mackie in pathology. We were told to call you with the John Doe results of the samples you sent to the lab."

"Yes?"

"Uh, okay. Yes, there is clear evidence of aggressive rabies infection. Quite frankly, I've never seen it this invasive. How long had it been from time of death to when this sample was collected?"

"I don't know, maybe ten minutes," Richard replied. There was silence on the line.

"Dr. Abercrombie, I have only seen this level of infection in research samples where the experiment was left for several weeks just to see what the upper limits of infection would be if the host were not first killed by the pathogen."

Mackie went on without waiting for a reply. "We hit it with the normal rabies vaccines and they were ineffective. Not sure what we have here. I'll have to file a report with the CDC. How would you like us to proceed?"

Richard rubbed his face; it was cold and wet.

"Uh, okay. Thank you, Dr. Mackie. Hold off on the report a couple of hours. Email me a copy of your results. I'll get back with you," he said, hanging up.

This was worse than he'd thought. They had a new strain here and didn't have anything to fight it if it ever came back.

Richard sat at his desk, staring at his hands. They hurt. No particular place, just inside. The conversation he had with Mackie was unsettling. He had been exposed to John Doe. The damned man had even splattered blood all over him and his staff. Strangely, it was almost if he could still feel the hot droplets scattered across his face.

It would be prudent to check himself in to the infectious disease ward until his tests came back. But if he did that, then he wouldn't be able to research as to what they needed to do if it did get passed to anyone else—himself or otherwise. And if this thing really had a two to three-hour incubation time, he'd be too far gone before the lab RT-PCR came back anyway. There was only one thing he could do.

He made his way to the dispensary. Good, the nurse wasn't on duty. To keep the virus from entering his central nervous system, or at least delay it a bit, he needed a rabies vaccine and a rabies immunoglobulin.

There. Two of each left.

One for himself and one for someone else. They just never saw these types of things up here, so why would they have very much on hand? He quickly placed them in his pocket and left for his office.

The click of his office door echoed in his ears. Quiet. Safe. He exhaled and the muscles in his shoulders relaxed a little. He needed a lot more of that. Taking a package out of this pocket, he administered the vaccine and immunoglobulin.

His phone buzzed.

Jesus Christ! Couldn't he get a moment's rest? It wasn't like there weren't several doctors on duty now. It was Dr. Chris Jamerson. Since he called Chris in, he should probably at least answer the phone.

"Yes?"

"Richard, this is Chris. Sorry to bother you 'cause you're probably trying to catch some shuteye, but we've got something weird going on down here in the recovery wards and ICU."

"What is it?" Richard snapped.

"The heart rate and body temps of all the unconscious patients are going up, the rest of the conscious traffic accident patients and half the staff are exhibiting some odd combination of flu-like symptoms with some type of hyper-nasal allergic response, and some folks are getting agitated for some reason. With the almost uncontrollable sneezing, they can barely take care of the patients. I know you've had similar symptoms, but the incubation rate seems way off. Any ideas?"

Oh shit…

The pieces began to fall into place. Transmission with abnormally fast incubation times…just like John Doe's rabies. Now his flu was spreading faster than normal. Increased agitation…

I hope to God these are at best coincidences, or even because of some common third infection agent…

"Richard?"

"Oh, yeah. I have to look into something. I'll get back with you shortly."

Richard threw open the door and ran to the dispensary, blowing past the nurse asking what he needed, and dug through one of the cabinets. With one smooth move, he flicked the syringe cap and pulled a generous amount of general anti-viral drug from the bottle and injected directly into the vein in his arm. Yes, he'd just taken the rabies anti-viral, but he needed to throw everything at this. Yanking it from his arm he drew another amount from the bottle.

"Doctor! What are you doing?" the nurse worriedly asked. "That needle's dirty and that is a dangerous amount of drugs to mainline all in one go."

"Yeah, like that's what's worrying me right now." He had to stay on top of this if there was to be any hope of containing whatever this is.

On his way back to his office he thumbed through the contact list on his phone and started calling other hospitals. They had to get as many inoculations going along with testing to stay ahead of this.

"This is Dr. Abercrombie of Mercy General. Do you have any extra PEP kits? No? Well, yeah we're all short staffed, and I know it's Christmas. Look, we have a situation and need some extra kits. Tomorrow at the earliest? Fine." But no matter how many calls he made, the answer was the same or worse.

Damn holiday.

Shit. Shit. Shit! What to do?

If he didn't make a big enough deal of this, then things could start unraveling quickly. If he overblew things too much and it turned out to be nothing, it would end his spiraling career that much faster.

Must think. Can't...mind won't connect the dots... Damn, my head is splitting open!

It was unclear if it was the pain or something else, but all the bright lights now had tracers. And the sound. The ticking of the clock felt as if it were coming from within his head, made by a little man sitting and banging a giant metal pan. Shit, maybe he should get an x-ray? Especially if there was someone in there causing the noise?

Jesus, I'm losing it! he thought, shaking his head to clear his thoughts, regretting it immediately.

Richard made his way back to the recovery wards, bumping into people who appeared out of nowhere and walls that jumped out in front of him. Screams got louder, echoing down the hallways. Sounded like they were coming from his destination or maybe hell...hard to tell.

When he arrived, nurses, doctors, and attendants were rushing around, trying to treat people in various states of duress, some screaming, some wandering around with glazed stares, some bloody and looking for something. It seemed more like a ninetieth century insane asylum on a bad day than Mercy General. What the hell was going on?

He had to contain this. Career be damned. He ran down the hall and grabbed one of the security guards heading to the mayhem.

"You! Come with me. We're locking this place down. Start with the two sets of doors on either side of the recovery ward."

"Sir?"

"Do it, damn it! Then report back to me at the front entrance. Call in your buddies and have them lock this place down tight. All exits! Don't let anyone out."

Richard made his way back to the nurse's station to see what he could learn. Sarah was there and looked rough.

"Shouldn't you have gone home by now?" he asked.

"Don't start with me, Hun—" she said before a sneezing fit overtook her.

Oh no. Not Sarah. Need to keep her with her head in the game. Can't do this without her.

He reached into his coat pocket and pulled out the last PEP kit, opened it and prepped the syringe.

Walking toward her he said, "Sarah, give me your arm."

Between sneezes she said, "Doc, have you lost your damn mind? You better keep that needle to yourself."

"Sarah, I don't have time for this. You've already contracted whatever this is and I won't be around long enough to keep things under control until help arrives."

With obvious distrust, she extended her arm and he injected her.

"Hey Richard, have you seen Cassie? Uh, what's going on?" asked Dave as he walked around the corner.

"Sorry Dave, I only had—" a loud crashed interrupted Richard. A chair clattered and skidded along the hallway, having been thrown through one of the locked doors to the recovery ward. The patients flowed out of the opening en masse, scrambling to get out, screaming and thrashing at each other and any nurse who might be nearby.

"Quick! Everyone to the NICU. We can lock the door there," ordered Richard.

The three rushed for the door and slammed it closed, using the emergency latches to secure it. They watched through the window as the screaming horde ran for the main exit, slamming against the door and bursting forth into the city. Gunshots rang out, but the security guards were only able to take two out before they were torn to pieces.

Richard became light-headed as he watched the rabid, infectious crowd pour out of the hospital. His stomach threatened to turn inside out at any moment. There was nothing he could do now. He'd failed. They'd lost containment. Only one thing to do now.

"Stay here." Richard rushed to the nearest elevator.

Got to get this information out!

What had he done? This was all because of him. Because he needed to be the damn martyr who was working over Christmas covering everyone's shifts. Covering the shifts just so he didn't have to deal with the reality that the alternative was him sitting at home alone. Having to admit that he didn't have anyone. No emotional connections with anyone. All because of his hubris?

Instead, he pushed himself, broke down his immune system, caught the flu, and kept freaking working. He was a doctor, for God's sake. There was no mystery that he got sick. Probably subconsciously made those decisions to ensure it happened so the holiday would be the most miserable possible, all the while covering shifts so others could be at home with their happy, perfect damn families.

He didn't expect to come face-to-face with a hyper-contagious rabies virus which would merge with his flu virus. But ignorant of it all, he kept working. Kept seeing patients because he was a goddamn doctor and knew what was best. He was so damn smart! Too good for this podunk little hospital. Too smart for a little virus.

He was responsible.

He was responsible for the infected, screaming throng that now roamed the streets of his city…maybe further. So many things he could have done, should have done differently, but didn't.

I'm sorry…

Richard typed away feverishly at his computer. The monitor, the only light in the room, washed his face in a sickening glow.

There. The CDC's email address. Dear…Sir? Mr. CDC? Think. Think! Why is this so hard? Maybe if my head would just explode already it might feel better! Should get Sarah to take the hammer she has in her bottom drawer and sink it right behind my ears. The crazy bitch would probably enjoy every second of it!

He rubbed his shaking hands over his cold, damp face.

Focus! Got to focus. Can't give in to it…

He proceeded to peck out a brief note and attach the few lab reports he had.

Ah! Can't stand it any longer. He feverishly rubbed his face.

The pain, the intensely itching pain! It was if there were ten thousand fire ants marching around on the inside of his skin with their tiny little damn feet. And with every other step they would stop and bite him with their freaking painful poison. And just for fun, a swarm of red wasps would join in and sting the living shit out of him every damn second. Over and over again every damn second!

Maybe if he could just peel off the damned itching burning skin that would feel better. Yes! That was an excellent idea! So easy, why hadn't he thought of that before? Oh, it would feel so good to get rid of it all!

He sat digging one sharp fingernail into the skin of his cheek. Oh, the tease of sweet relief.

Not yet, must finish the email first.

…it is an aggressive form of rabies that has now gone airborne, likely through mutation incorporating influenza DNA with its own, using the sneezing mechanism to spread more efficiently from host to host. Instead of taking days to weeks to manifest into acute stages, it now is one to two hours. And for preventative measures there is no way to be able to distinguish between the symptoms of influenza until it's too late.

The primary symptoms are typical pain and disorientation associated with the rabies virus. It makes the infected incredibly dangerous as the virus seems to be attacking the fight or flight centers of the brain with unbelievable pain. The infected are very dangerous, irrational, only wanting to lash out violently, and will likely continue until they give out due to exposure, dehydration, heart failure from elevated heart rate, or bleed out due to mortal injuries.

It is unfortunate more information is not available, but it is my medical opinion that our city should be isolated with a kill-zone perimeter at all costs. However, it is quite possible the virus can jump species freely. Best of luck. I'm sorry I couldn't do more. But maybe I did enough…

Dr. R. Abercrombie.

Sounds of screams of fear in equal measure to those of abject pain and anger grew louder, not only in the hospital but also outside in the streets, along with car alarms, horns and crashing vehicles. If only he hadn't been so arrogant and proud. What will the ultimate cost be to not only himself and the rest of the world? What would they have to do to stop this?

Screw it! What do I care? Let this messed up world burn!

The room filled with the guttural howl of an animal. Had one of the infected patients gotten in? Was it an infected animal looking for a kill? It didn't matter.

Touching his burning face, it was clear it came from his own open, contorted mouth.

He was losing his grip…on everything. Probably should document the advanced symptoms from a doctor's perspective so that it might help them. His last gift. Documenting his own selfish creation.

Ahhhh!

His brain was on fire with the marching, biting ants, sending bolts of fiery lightning throughout his body, locking it in a perpetual, ridged spasm. Unknown moments passed, locked with every muscle of his body angrily seized trying to rip themselves free of their bony bonds.

Then relief. Exhausting relief.

He fumbled for a piece of paper and a pen. There was no way he would be able to type now. Best hope would be to scrawl something out.

To whom it may concern. The advanced symptoms appear to be an attack of the primary nerve pathways via the central nervous system typical of rabies virus. Intense pain, disorientation, aggression towards…anything. Sensory overload, miserable flu-like symptoms, and a desire to peel my skin off.

Maybe that last part was too much, but oh, how wonderful the release would feel.

Aahhh! Uuuuuu….

Another spasm set fire to the inside of his back then released him from its grip.

Fingers searched for the particularly bothersome spot on his face. Searching for the place where it burned the most. There! Nails dug in, pressing through the rubbery layer of fire, wasps, and ants. Pressing deeper so he could get a hold of the bothersome skin. Already, some relief! With a slow, deliberate, steady pull, a strip of cheek peeled away. Oh, mother of God that felt good, the icy pain of the skin letting go of itself washed away the fire of the ants! Oh shit! Relief! Before the night was over, he would get rid of it all, if it would bring this wonderful release.

Must write that down. No. That will be their surprise. Just sign the letter.

The intensifying sounds and screams associated with the world falling apart outside his office echoed into his consciousness once again. He positioned his hand over the paper and signed 'Abercrombie'.

Hmm, Forgot 'doctor'.

As he wrote 'Dr.', another spasm locked his body in its grasp causing a scream to escape his mouth.

As it released, he noticed on the letter where he tried to sign his name when the pain hit, he'd drawn a large squiggled line through the first part of Abercrombie. Now it looked more like 'Zombie'.

Somewhere in the back of his mind, a small voice laughed bitterly.

The world collapsed into a narrow tunnel before him. Thoughts moved slowly and flashes of pain illuminated the world.

A blood-curdling scream escaped his chest. He stood, rushed to the door, and swung it open with such force it embedded the handle into the wall, then rushed out into the chaos.

The Butcher Boy
Amira K. Makansi & Jessica West

Small-town ruffienne Charlotte Adams isn't one to back down from a challenge, and the rumors of a ghost in the woods near her home are too much of a temptation.

WHISPERS FLUTTERED AROUND the schoolyard like the ribbons the girls tied into their hair.

"Johnny said he saw one last night."

"Saw what?"

"One of old Conrad's sons. The Butcher Boy."

"What'd he look like?"

"Ask Johnny yuh-self. I ain't gon' speak about them boys."

Charlotte had already gone grave-robbing with her older brother and last month met an escaped Negro slave on the Railroad. She knew what darkness the world held and she didn't believe in ghosts or dead men anywhere but six feet under. She was bold. So she sauntered up to

Johnny Fairwell with a smirk on her face and asked him what Conrad Butcher's dead son looked like.

"Like a pun-kin," Johnny responded, fear in his eyes, but not from Charlotte. "Ridin' a great big horse, with a bone knife in 'is hand. Had a smile carved to his face what looked to be done with that same blade."

"Where you seen him?"

"Out by the mill pond where them thieves shot him last year."

"I don' believe you."

"You callin me a liar, Charlotte Adams?"

"I'm sayin' you saw a funny-lookin' tree and thought it was a dead man, Johnny."

Boys and girls hissed and cawed around Johnny as he leapt at Charlotte, fire in his eyes. But at nine years old with an older brother who'd showed her the world, Charlotte was the fiercest ruffian in town. She ducked under Johnny's outstretched arm and tackled him from behind. She bit into his shoulder, tasting dirt and iron as he bled into her mouth. She had him on the ground a second later, but when she felt a rough hand on the back of her dress she knew she'd been outdone. Miss Morris, the schoolteacher, was the only face Charlotte had any fear of.

After a half-hour of kneeling in the corner as punishment for her crimes, Charlotte had thought of plenty of ways to get back at the boy responsible for this injustice. But the seed of curiosity had slipped inside of her, and the image of the Butcher Boy with a smile sliced into his face had caught her imagination. Some part of her believed. Some part of her wanted to see it.

And so, when the bell rang at the end of the day, Charlotte chased Johnny halfway up the street to catch him.

"I ain't gone hit a girl 'gain," he said as soon as he saw her. "Turner says it's bad luck."

"You hit me or don't, see if I care. But I bet you ain't brave enough to take me out where you saw that Butcher ridin'."

"First you call me a liar and now a coward?"

"So, prove you ain't neither," she sang. "Take me there tonight afore he rides off ta some other town."

Johnny shrugged, trying to look unconcerned. But Charlotte could see the fear in his eyes. She's seen it in the eyes of the men she'd gone digging with. She'd seen it in the eyes of the Negro on his way North. Fear excited her. Fear was a challenge. Fear was an adventure.

"All right then," Johnny said, capitulating. He squinted into the blue sky as if trying to see something there. "You meet me by the creek at half past ten. You tell a soul what I gon' show you, I'll kill you my own self."

"I'd like to see you try," she retorted. But inwardly she was reveling. "I'll be there." She grinned at him. "Don't be afraid, Johnny. Dead men cain't hurt you."

Johnny shrugged.

Half past ten was a tight squeeze for Charlotte to make it all the way down to the creek. She had no trouble staying up so late, as she did so every night anyway, unbeknownst to her folks. Most times these days she spent the time playing games with her dolls in the shadows. But when her brother was around and if the moon was full, they'd sneak out together and find an adventure. That was how come she was the bravest of any child in town her age. But since her parents had sent her brother away to school, her evenings had become decidedly dull. Tonight would be a rare treat.

The tricky part of it was that her parents went to bed at ten on the dot. Pa'd start snoring in ten minutes, if not less. Ma, though, would read her Farmer's Almanac by the bedside oil lamp for a while yet.

Charlotte hopped out of bed at five past and tiptoed into the kitchen, sitting on the worn wood floor in front of the pantry, near their bedroom door.

At ten past, her pa let loose with the first of his sawin'. That's what her ma had always called it. Said he "sawed logs" in his sleep.

At twenty after, Ma turned out the light. It'd be another few minutes before she'd drift off. Even so, Charlotte reckoned she could slip out the back door and her folks'd be none the wiser.

Out the back door and down the steps, Charlotte checked the full moon high up in the night sky. Plenty of light up here where the trees kept their distance from the house, but down through the brush was another matter.

In her nightshirt and boots, Charlotte rushed to the edge of the thick woods that led downhill to the creek that ran behind their home. A thrill of excitement rushed through her at the prospect of catching a glimpse of the Butcher Boy.

He'd sliced up one of those thieves pretty good before they shot him. The man still wore the scars Billy gave him that day. They said the thieves had cut up his face as he lay dying, the same as he did to anyone who crossed him, but ole Mr. Conrad came upon the scene before they could finish him off. They never did find his body. All that was left were rumors of a moonshine factory a ways downstream of the creek behind Charlotte's house. After the first deputy to search the area turned up dead—a gruesome grin sliced into his face—they stopped lookin'.

If the ghost of Billy Butcher was anywhere, she was sure they'd find him there.

She stopped just shy of the tree line at the edge of their property, gazing into the thick brush beyond. She drew up short at how dark it was in those woods. Briefly, she contemplated going back for her doll. But she knew if she showed up at the creek with her Lucy in hand, that ole Johnny Fairwell would give her what for and her reputation in town would be ruined.

She straightened her spine and told herself what her pa had told her a million times before if he'd told her once. "Tighten up, girl. Get to the work of gettin' it done." The sound of her voice, though pale compared to the hoot owl in the trees, made her feel a little better.

She reached out for the spindly tree with the roots that made a short set of steps that wound in a circle like the fancy staircase in the military school where her brother was. One, two, three, four steps 'round the sturdy sapling then she glanced back at her house, barely able to see it from where she now stood.

Light from the moon filtered through the trees. The shadows dripped like oil onto her nightshirt and moved across her as she walked away from home, toward the creek. Every step brought her deeper into the darkness, further away from the light, and closer to the Butcher Boy.

Charlotte looked back, but couldn't see home anymore. She could just barely make out the tree with the step-roots. She'd made this trip a thousand and one times during the day, but for a brief moment, she wondered if she'd be able to find her way to the creek or back home in the pitch of night.

Damned if she'd turn back now, though. Johnny would never let her hear the end of it. But the thick brush between her and the creek was awful dark. Her heart picked up the pace, even as her feet slowed.

To get to the creek, she'd have to pass through the tall reedy grasses that howled in the wind and whipped her when properly riled. And the wind was howlin' right proper tonight, bet your bottom dollar.

She stopped and stood at a flat patch of ground—the last place she'd see light if she kept going, until she reached the wide creek—facing what she knew to be a ten-minute trek through the reeds.

"Aw, hell," she said. Her voice trembled so much that she was glad that stupid boy wasn't here with her. Kind of. "He probably ain't even there." Her mind made up against this foolishness, Charlotte turned to go back home.

A little boy's terrified scream lit up her mind like flint had struck tinder right before her eyeballs, leaving behind a vision of Johnny with a wide, bloody grin splitting his face in two.

Charlotte jumped, spun around, and raced back to the tree, up the little stair, back to her moon-lit home. She was crying and shaking by the time she made it to the back steps. But before she barged right in, she paused.

Pa would turn her across his lap for sure if she woke 'em at this hour and told 'em she was to meet Johnny at the creek. Not that she was scared of a whoopin', mind you, but if Johnny was playing a prank on her, she'd get that whipping for nothing.

Charlotte strained to listen for another scream—any sound really—but she had no way of knowing if she could even hear him all the way from here. She went in quietly through the back door, tip toed into the kitchen, and sat on the floor again.

The clock over the mantle showed a quarter of eleven. Charlotte rocked back and forth for a moment, hugging her knees and wishing, once again, she had her doll. She hadn't even been gone thirty minutes, but who knew how long Johnny had been down at the creek waiting for her? That scream hadn't sounded fake, either. Much as she hated to admit it, she'd never forgive herself if Johnny died and hadn't even tried to help him.

Charlotte, wet faced and filthy, opened the door to her parents' bedroom and whispered, "Ma?" She cleared her throat—another tremor racked her frame—and whined, "Mama."

Her mother didn't stir.

"Mama," she said again, more loudly, even as she flinched at the sound of her own voice against the still of the house.

This time, her mother stirred, turned over, and blinked against the darkness.

"What's the matter, love?"

"I—I think you need to come down to the creek, Mama," Charlotte stammered. "I just heard a scream and I think someone's in trouble."

Her father muttered something in his sleep, then sat up abruptly, his narrowed eyes striking more fear into Charlotte's heart than the screams of any man.

"You go on back to bed now, you hear?"

"But, Papa," she whined.

"I ain't heard no noise and you wakin' us at this time of night is causing nothing but trouble. I don't wanna hear about you getting into no more messes with that damned brother of yours."

A shudder ran up and down Charlotte's spine as she heard a second scream. Less of a scream, this time, than a howl—the sound of a hound on a scent, perhaps, or the cry of a tortured animal. But her father's face showed no recognition.

"Papa! Ain't you heard that noise?" Her voice just barely creaked out over the whispers and strains of their old house.

"You having dreams and nightmares, child," her mother said gently. "Go back to sleep."

The sound ringing in her ears, Charlotte crept away, chastised. She thought she was imagining things. But when she heard the third cry, she knew this was her demon to face and hers alone. A bolt of courage leapt through her as she realized she'd possibly led Johnny to the creek and then abandoned him to the hands of an angry ghost. She dashed to her room, grabbed not her doll but her skinning knife, a birthday present last year from her brother, and sprinted out the door. The door slammed against its old frame behind her, but Charlotte was so far down the path she hardly heard it.

As she raced down to the creek, she twisted and turned through the arms of bushes and vines that grabbed at her as she tore past. The night was bright and moonlit, but wisps of fog drifted around her, and Charlotte trembled even as she ran. She unsheathed her blade even as she remembered her brother's words of caution— "You'll fall and kill yourself"—and held it out in front of her like a talisman as she stumbled towards her meeting point with Johnny.

She emerged through the brush to the creek, lush with water and foliage, and she listened again for the cries that had drawn her here. Even over the sounds of her own heavy breathing, the silence was deafening. "Johnny?" Charlotte called as loudly as she dared.

Hoo! an owl cried back.

Charlotte saw, downstream, the shape of a horse with a rider on its back.

"The Butcher Boy," she whispered, her voice floating down the creek on a tendril of fog. The rider turned his horse and brought the animal pacing upstream, towards where Charlotte stood half-hidden in the trees. The fear she'd felt earlier in the evening was gone, though her body quaked without her permission.

The horse stalked closer. Through the fog, Charlotte could just make out the man's face: the bright young eyes of Billy Butcher, old Conrad's dead son. Johnny was no liar. There was a smile carved into his cheeks from ear to ear, and Charlotte could see his eyes alight hungrily on her.

The leather saddle creaked when the Butcher Boy leaned over and swung down off his horse, splashing into the shallow stream just a few paces away. He turned to face Charlotte full-on. Moonlight glinted off a machete hanging at his right hip. Charlotte's useless pocket knife fell out of her numb fingers and onto the sandy creek shore at her feet.

Her knees locked. Though her thundering heart set her limbs to trembling, she couldn't move. Tears stung her eyes, which were frozen open like her mouth. Beyond the dark figure, she could just make out the shape of Johnny laying with his legs in the shallow water of the creek. She couldn't tell from this far if he was still breathing. She finally blinked and tried to scream. She licked her lips and took a deep breath, only to freeze again when the Butcher Boy sprang into action.

He reached her in three strides and clamped one hand down over her mouth. He grabbed her shoulder and gave her a good, firm shake. His breath reeked of garlic and tobacco, and some bitter, harsh chemical. Stained spittle dripped like venom from his teeth. He spoke clearly, but kept his deep, rough voice low. "Don't scream."

Every instinct in the little girl protested, assuring her that if ever there was a time to scream, this was it. But she just stood there, nodding as best she could beneath his grip. Her shaking subsided when he released her. Though she was still too scared to move, much less run, an odd, detached calm had come over her as she examined his features.

Though the moon shone full above the wide creek bed, the twinkling glare off the shallow waters did more to blind her to, rather than illuminate, the figure crouched before her. She could see him well enough. The grin that stretched across his face was a dark pink, jagged scar. Not the bloody, gaping tear she'd imagined. His glazed eyes shone like Papa's did when he was in his cups.

Charlotte bolstered her courage and regained some of the pluck that the ruffienne was known for. She raised her chin up, as pride demanded, and waited for the man to explain himself.

"I imagine you get thrown across your pa's knee often enough." He mumbled something about pity for her pa. Still crouching before her, he scratched the scruff on his chin as though considering what to do with her.

Her resolve of a moment before began to falter. Billy Butcher wasn't a ghost, but he was a full-grown man who had Johnny laid out on the sandy shore of the creek. A man she had to get past if she hoped to bring Johnny and herself home safe. If Johnny was still alive. Though she'd wrestled with her big brother enough times, the bigger he got, the less she won. But damned if she'd go down without a fight.

She was just about ready to mount an attack, spreading her feet and bending at the knees a bit. Billy saw her move into a battle stance and leaned closer.

"Think twice, little cowgirl." His voice mocked her. "I don't know what you hope to accomplish, but if you ever had a fighting chance, it weren't here and now." He stood up and gripped the reins of his horse, moving out of her line of sight to Johnny.

"If I'd wanted to you dead, you would be. Your friend there is knocked out. You and him can go, but you listen to me first. And if you take a swing at me, this'll be your last rodeo."

Charlotte waited to see if he'd really let them go, still prepared to fight to the death.

"What's your name, kid?"

"Charlotte Adams."

"Everybody thinks I'm dead, don't they?"

"Yeah."

Billy nodded, scratching his scruff some more. He met her eyes. "Good. Keep it that way."

She'd fought the roughest and toughest in her schoolyard, but this was no child. Billy Butcher was big, mind you, but so were her brother and her pa. The Butcher Boy wasn't much bigger than either, really. "You ain't no ghost, neither."

He pulled his machete and brought it level with her widened eyes.

"There are worse things in the woods than ghosts, Charlotte Adams. If you or any of your friends come back here again, I'll go visit your Ma and Pa and show you what a real monster looks like. You know what I done to them thieves that shot me?"

Charlotte gulped and nodded.

He replaced his machete, and mounted his horse. "Get your friend and go on home." Without another word, he crossed the shallow creek and found a niche in the thick foliage on the other side from which to supervise Charlotte's departure.

She rushed over to Johnny, who was just waking up. Groaning, he sat up, his legs soaking in the cool water while sand tumbled down his back from his hair. He looked over Charlotte's shoulder and froze.

"Bbbb...bbb…"

"Hush up now, Johnny." The authority in her voice stopped his blubbering. She had his attention, but Johnny was scared. "Don't you pay him no mind. He ain't gone do nothin'."

Charlotte started at the stamping hoof of the great, dark horse. Imagined the puffs of smoke that rose from his nostrils when he huffed at her affront.

"So long as we don't mess with him," she amended. Since he hadn't killed her outright, she was certain the Butcher Boy would hold true to his word. Either way, she'd die before she'd let Johnny see her fear of Billy Butcher.

"Now listen here, Johnny." Charlotte held Johnny's eyes, and did her very best imitation of Miss Morris. "I took care of us for now, but we cain't never come back here again."

Johnny took her hand and she pulled him to his feet.

Billy Butcher's giant horse pawed the ground and snorted, and Charlotte turned to look at him one last time. In the shadow of his hat, the only thing she could see of him was the grinning pink scar and his glowing eyes, lit up strangely by the moonlight.

She suppressed a shiver. He nodded silently as she turned away. She wrapped one of Johnny's arms around her shoulder and turned to walk him back upstream toward town.

"There's worse things at this here creek than ghosts, Johnny. Don't you ever come back here."

"Charlotte Adams," Johnny said, leaning against her, "you are wise as you are brave."

The Lacemaker
Daniel Arthur Smith

MY MORNING WALK is my favorite part of the day, because to me, that is when the Lions Meadow is most tranquil. I suppose that since the dome is a controlled environment, that sounds silly. But that's the time when the dew drops glisten and the birdsong is sweetest. Over the course of the last century, the path of my morning walk has veered little, varying over time for the growth of a tree and other maturations of the gardens. Apart from a blossoming orchid, the morning of Amory Willinputt's arrival was no different than any that had come before. I awoke, ate a breakfast of fresh tomato and melon as I watched the sun rise over the lake, then went out for my daily exercise. I'd finished my morning walk a few minutes early and come to the end of the drive to greet the new guest. The hover car rounded the curve promptly at 10:15, then slowed to a stop at the gate.

Then it just sat there.

I straightened my back and adjusted my head so that my long red braid floated between my shoulder blades then settled in the middle. This maneuver was partly to steal a glimpse through the tinted windows. I couldn't see through them of course, but the peripheral view of my own reflection forced me to muster a smile.

I wasn't sure what to expect of the new guest. I'd read the dossier labeled 'Amory Willinputt', but the data only revealed so much. He was a chemist, an important man—important to the syndicate anyway, important enough that they deemed him worthy of the procedure. But that was the only commonality of each and every guest.

A minute had passed, and the car still stood silent in the speckled morning light.

Thoughts of Ms. Garrant, a guest from two seasons before, flooded my mind. Ms. Garrant was a MidHi syndicate exec who must have read somewhere that making people wait was a power move, or maybe it was simply that she was a cold woman who lived for the grand entrance. I was about to resign myself to the reality of another such guest when the gull panel door raised up and a thin young man stepped out. Everything about him was restrained. His sandy hair was pulled back tight. He sucked in his cheeks and held his chin aristocratically up and away from me so that his emerald green eyes looked past me and onto the surroundings—another silly power move. He was oddly dressed for the warm country morning. He wore a long velvet coat, the color of chocolate, tapered at his waist, and beneath it a bright white shirt with a crisp mandarin collar, buttoned to the top. With the age mods, he appeared perhaps twenty, but the dossier had disclosed his true age as four times that.

I wasn't in the least put off. I've been greeting guests at the gate for decades. Sometimes it's like a staring contest. Sooner or later the guest will cave. I waited until he glanced at me to greet him. "Mr. Willinputt," I said. "Welcome to the Lions Meadow. I'm your host, Imogen Cain."

"Hello Ms. Cain," he said. His response wasn't unkind, but it was distracted and drawn out, his eyes caught up in the highest branches of the nearby poplars. "Please, call me Amory."

"It's Miss. But Imogen will do fine. I trust your travel was pleasant."

"Quite uneventful," he said, his eyes moving to a tall pine. "I must say, this is so impressive. I've never seen anything...quite...like it."

"Thank you," I said, undeterred. Again, I was used to this reaction. "We're quite proud of our gardens. Though some guests find the sheer nature of the facility overwhelming. If you'll please follow me."

Willinputt breathed in a deep breath and released it. "Even the air," he said. "So fresh."

I was peripheral to his attention. But, so be it. Men like Amory expected deference from those around them. In my opinion, that's adolescent, but there was no reason for me not to be polite.

"The dome is a self-reliant biosphere. If you'll follow me," I said again. "I'll escort you to your room to freshen up. Then we'll lunch and tour the grounds."

Amory gestured behind him toward the car. "What about my—"

"Your luggage will be taken ahead of us and placed in your room. You didn't bring too much, did you?"

"No," he said. "Just what I might need after the procedure."

With that the gull door fell closed and the hover car silently glided toward the service drive.

The house was mere meters away, down a gradual hill. Amory didn't appear to have taken notice of it yet.

"The blue sky, the green leaves," he said. "I wouldn't have believed that a vivarium could appear so natural if I hadn't seen it with my own eyes."

"I'm sorry to disappoint you," I said as I led him toward the house. "I mentioned the dome was self-reliant, but that is misleading. It's a closed system. But a good portion of what you see is artificial."

"The trees aren't real?"

"The trees are. The grass. But the blue sky, the clouds—they're provided by resonators embedded in the ceiling of the dome."

"And the birds?" he said, with a note of disappointment. "I suppose they're synthetic too."

I gave him an apologetic shrug, and the vigor returned to his face.

"Still," he said. "It's unbelievable. What a contrast to the Meg."

"It's a benefit to the procedure, for most anyway."

"I can see that. I'm already at ease, happier." His eyes dropped to meet mine. "You've undergone the procedure?"

"You're asking because of my eyes."

"Yes. You're not a synthetic?" he asked, focusing closer on my face.

"What if I told you they were naturally blue?"

"But they are so blue. They're natural?"

"Not at all. The procedure was necessary in order for me to perform my role. Of course, it was so long ago, it's like my eyes were always this way."

"You're the lacemaker?"

"Yes. I am."

"You know I'd never imagined, short of a catastrophic accident, that I'd be a candidate."

"Don't sell yourself short," I said. "The work you've done for the syndicate is beyond reproach."

He responded with an agreeable nod. But in fact I had no idea what it was that Amory did, just that it must have been important.

"Maples and roses," he said as we approached the door. He was referring to line of rare ornamental trees and bushes beneath the windows.

"You're familiar?" I asked.

"Yes. I've seen these before, in a small solarium."

"Syndicate?"

"Yes. How did you know—" then he caught himself. "Oh, right."

I opened the door and led him in. The entrance opened to a staircase, but his attention was immediately drawn to the high open room off to the right.

"Post and beam?" he said. His eyes, again, focused above. "Real wood?"

"Synthetic," I said. "My father taught me that it was better to be subtle. I find it intimate despite its size." I led him around the stairwell into the great room. I watched his eyes follow the ceiling beams above the door as they angled across the room to the top of a two-story windowed wall.

"Your father...it slipped past me before," he said, "Cain."

"Yes," I said. My family name was synonymous with wealth. It was my grandfather who had succeeded in securing our position in the syndicate, something seldom discussed. Fortunately, Amory's attention had already shifted to was what was beyond the glass.

"Oh, my," Amory said as he walked past me. "What an amazing view. The trees out front were fantastic, spectacular even, but this lake..." Beyond the wall was a red-tiled solarium, two meters deep, and beyond the second glass wall, a lake nearly a mile across, surrounded by an oak and maple forest. When he reached the glass, he stopped. "How large is the dome exactly?"

"Again. I'm sorry to disappoint. What you're seeing is a projection. Beyond that wall is the power station and the storage facility."

"But the way the light is entering the solarium...It looks so..." Amory appeared to be searching for the right word.

"Real?" I offered.

"Yes. Real."

"Well. It is, in that it exists, or existed, somewhere. But does that make a difference if the experience is the same?"

"I suppose not," he said. "I suppose that after the procedure, I'll have to get used to it."

"Well, that is best, for your sake. Let me show you to your room."

The ceiling above creaked with the weight of Amory's steps. He had awoken. With the exception of the soft tangerine light emanating from the workstation embedded in the surface of my desk, the main hall was dark. I rose from my seat and went to the small table I'd set up in front of the darkened two-story solarium. On the table were two silver trays: one held a pitcher of orange juice, a small carafe of water, and two large champagne flutes; the other tray held a syringe, three pastel colored tablets, and a rocks glass. And resting beside them in a bucket of ice, a corked bottle of champagne.

I waited, hands crossed, for him to enter the room.

It's common for guests to be closer to their best selves after a rest. Traveling to the Lions Meadow is arduous, even in the luxury of a hover car. When Amory entered the hall, I immediately recognized a change. His physical appearance had certainly undergone a transformation. Without the tapered coat, the billow of his white shirt added a girth to his slender frame, and his hair, no longer pulled back tight, rested wistfully on his shoulders. But it was his demeanor that appeared most transformed. I can best describe it as a calmness that had set about him.

"Good afternoon, Amory," I said in my most enthusiastic hostess voice. "I trust you're rested."

"Yes," he said. "I didn't realize it was dark already."

"Oh," I said. "It's not quite night. I dimmed the view while you rested. Lilly, the lake please." On my command, the outer solarium wall illuminated. An unseen sun was setting to the right, casting a band of gold across the treetops to the left side of the lake. Near the shore, three green headed wood ducks swam past, the golden shimmer of the reflected two-tone forest wavering in their wake.

"Amazing," he said. "This exists, or existed, somewhere?"

"Yes. Shall we have a cocktail?"

"If you insist," he said, his attention still fixed on the water.

"Well, It's actually the next step in the procedure. But there's no reason why we shouldn't make it enjoyable."

I poured the contents of the carafe into the rocks glass then plopped the three tablets in, one at a time. The tablets furiously fizzed in reaction to the water.

"Potassium and glucose," he said.

"And few other pick-me-ups," I said, handing him the orange drink they created. "It helps the procedure along."

Amory poured the contents down his throat and returned the glass to me.

I set it on the tray then picked up the syringe.

Amory put his hand up. "Will it hurt?"

"The syringe?" I asked. "No. There's no needle. A magnetically activated actuator releases a hypo-spray." I squinted playfully. "You know this. You won't feel a thing."

"Not that. I mean the procedure. The lace. Will it hurt?"

"On the contrary. The procedure is designed to stimulate your pleasure centers. You'll find it quite enjoyable."

"Okay," he said.

"Okay," I agreed. But I could tell by the shortness of his answer that he wasn't convinced. "Just turn around for a second…and tilt your head forward."

A soft hiss signaled the release of the syringe's contents into the back of his neck.

Amory reached up to rub the spot as he turned back around.

"See," I said. "That wasn't so bad."

I immediately filled the two flutes a third of the way up with orange juice, added the bubbling champagne, then offered him one. "Cheers," I said as I raised my glass.

"Cheers," he responded, then sipped the mimosa. He was quiet for a moment, peering out over the virtual lake.

I ran my finger up and down the side of my glass, then I too turned my gaze to the lake. These contemplative moments were expected from new guests. The beverage

I'd given Amory contained calming agents and it was most always an immediate response for the guest to process the procedure. This clarity opened pathways for the neural dust, which in turn boosted the brain's chemical receptors, leading to a euphoric state.

It did not take long for Amory. "So what now?" he asked.

"I introduce you to Prospero."

"Who's Prospero?"

"Lilly, let's visit Prospero," I said, issuing the auditory command to change the projection. The view of the lake beyond the solarium's outer glass faded to black. The unmistakable sound of underwater bubbles, followed by a series of dolphin clicks and whistles, filled the room. The high wall began to faintly glow turquoise. The entire wall rippled as it grew brighter. A school of small silver fish raced beneath a flickering ray of sunlight. The pursuer entered the vista from the right: a dolphin with glowing cerulean eyes.

"Prospero," I beckoned.

The dolphin somersaulted then spun to face me. From speakers hidden high up in the thick wooden beams came more clicks and whistles, then a playful voice. "Imogen. How's tricks?"

"Quite all right, thank you," I said. "I see you're enjoying a run."

"Well, I can't actually feed in here, but I do enjoy the frolic of the hunt."

"I bet you do. Listen, I called you up because we have some work to do later this evening."

"Delightful. Is this our guest?" She thrashed her tail and spun toward Amory.

"This is Amory," I said.

"Hi, Amory."

He was in awe. "Amazing," he said again.

A series of whistles squealed from the speakers, followed by, "Why thank you. You're quite amazing as well, Mister Chemistry."

"Interactive," he said, "real time. And a dolphin."

"Prospero," I said, "is not really a dolphin. She is a Librarian with the Archive. She exists in the frame, a subset of the archive."

"She's a virtual synthetic?"

"No. She's human. She's just interfaced—"

"Is this what the lace will do to me?"

Clicks and whistles. "No, silly," said Prospero.

"Prospero is part of an organic bioinformatic system," I said.

"An organic computational system?" Amory asked.

"Yes," I said. "Prospero is a true bioinformatic system. A person interfaced with bio organisms. This allows an immense degree of processing power. She'll assist me in designing the lace work."

Clickety-click. "An immense degree. Ha, ha, ha." Prospero somersaulted again, then disappeared to the surface.

Amory's brows deepened. "If she's not a dolphin, why surface?"

"She doesn't need to breathe if that's what you're asking. She doesn't like to hover as she communicates with the archive."

"Why the dolphin at all?"

"She's adventurous."

"I'd heard rumors that the Archive wasn't a mere AI. That is was a human driven system."

"It's not a deep secret. The Librarians know, of course."

"Why share the secret with me?"

"You'll know after the procedure anyway. With the lace, you'll have direct access to the Archive."

Amory nodded, sipped from his mimosa, then said, "I'm familiar with the Bard. Prospero is such an interesting name."

"Kay."

"Excuse me?"

"Her name is Kay. She uses the nickname Prospero because to her, it means island wizard."

"Ah," said Amory. "She fancies herself a wizard."

"Well, she is currently a dolphin."

Thin bars, wands of bright tangerine light, shot out from the glowing thimbles on each of my fingertips as my hands darted around the transparent sphere mounted above my desk. Within the sphere, I expertly manipulate an iridescent purple mist. With each rise or fall of a finger, the purple cloud flickered and contorted.

"You have lighting in a bottle," said Amory. He was reclining in a soft leather chaise, facing the two-story-high solarium.

The wands of light disappeared from my fingers as I sat back to observe the sphere. "It is like a lightning storm, I suppose."

"Ah," Amory sighed sweetly. "It reminds me of a plasma lamp I had as a child. Except the lighting in the lamp burst from an electrode in the center. Not in a cloud like that."

"It's radically different," I said. "But I suppose it's based on the same technology. I thought I lost you there for a bit."

"I was watching Prospero herd a small school of fish to and fro across the grand aquarium span across the outer wall. Quite enjoyable."

"Yes. It is."

"What is it you that you're doing exactly?" he asked.

"You studied the procedure?"

"Yes. But what exactly are you doing now?"

"I'm placing the neural dust that I injected into your system."

"I thought the neural dust found its own path."

"Do you know what the neural dust is?"

"Nanos, right? Crystal-based, like all of the quantum tech."

"That's right. Each mote is a piezoelectric crystal, smaller than a splinter. Piezoelectric means—"

"That they produce a small charge. I'm a chemist."

"Right again," I said. My fingertips ignited and once again the bright orange wands shot into the sphere. "So that charge will ultimately assist the neural lace, but in the meantime, those splinters—the neural dust, if you will—perform a few different tasks. They map the neurons upon which the lacework is created, and in the progress, seek out vessels with potential weak spots—which they stint."

"So that sphere is—"

"A mirror," I said. "The contents of the sphere mirror the contents of your head." I tapped the globe and a deeper purple, three-dimensional image superimposed over the rolling mist.

"That's my brain," said Amory.

"Yes," I said. I tapped the sphere a second time with a different finger combination and a red, three-dimensional webbing filled the brain. "And this is your vascular system."

"Outstanding. And you're manipulating all of this…neural dust?"

"Oh, no. There are far too many for me to even contemplate." I tapped the sphere yet a third time and the brain and vascular system disappeared. "That's where Prospero comes in. She assists in identifying optimal points to anchor the neural lace. For her, it's near effortless."

"You said 'potential weak spots'."

"The neural lace increases blood flow. Your age mods maintain vascular structure, but the stints ensure the paths are open and won't suffer stress."

"I don't remember that being a predominant risk factor."

"It's not at all, really. Perhaps it was at one time, but now it's compensated for in the procedure. While Prospero's in there, she runs scenarios to ensure that the stints are properly placed."

"Oddly, I'm not concerned about it at all."

I smiled. At this point in the procedure, the serotonin and dopamine were firing heavy. He wouldn't mind being tossed from a plane.

"You'll be tired soon. You may not realize it, but there's a lot going on in your cranium right now. Lay back and close your eyes."

The beams shooting from my fingertips were now a bright electric blue—different thimbles for a different purpose. In repetition, my fingers elongated and contracted in a rolling motion from my pointer to my pinky, my right-hand mirroring my left, so that they appeared to be squeezing the air above the sphere. The wands of light told the true tale, as they wove hairline strands of metal and plastic together into neural lace.

The undersea vista beyond the second set of panes was gone, replaced by the late-night sky. The thin tree line above the lake faintly defined itself against a ceiling of indigo, and hovering in its midst, the morning star.

"Hesperus is Phosphorus," said Amory. His voice was course.

"And both are the planet Venus," I said. "There's some water next to you."

"Ah," he said. "Thank you."

Amory leaned forward and poured the contents of the carafe into a tall thin glass, then drank the entirety in one quaff.

"Ah," he said again, this time absent the rasp. "The elixir of water. Where did Prospero go?"

"Anywhere and everywhere. She left after we finished mapping the neural dust. She has to repeat the task elsewhere. The lacework falls on me."

"It looks like you're kneading dough," he said. His eyes were wide and there was a slight slur to his words. "But with long blue needles."

"I see you're still feeling elated."

"Elated is a good word. Drunk may be another. But I'm not drunk. In fact, my mind is clear. I feel…like I'm in my twenties again. I feel…alive. Invincible. It'll be a shame when the chemicals wear off."

"If it counts for anything, there's no hangover. I think you'll find that you're a new man."

"Ha, ha. I will be. Do you know why I'm getting this procedure?"

"Sure. You're an important chemist."

"Yes. Not that important, but a chemist. It's quite actually hush, hush. But I'm compelled to share."

"One of the reasons we conduct the protocol in isolation is to ensure hush, hush."

"Ah. That is smart. You know what I'm about to tell you?"

"Yes. But feel free."

A wide smile crept across Amory's face. "You see, there's a Syndicate City on Roxon II. That's a mid-sized rock on the edge of the colonies. The city has a name, but it doesn't matter."

"It doesn't?"

"Well. I suppose that after the procedure it will. The city is called Lewan. It was named after the first Governor, Jan Lewandowski. He went by Lewan."

"I see."

"Anyway, the miners there have made a discovery, what may be a profound discovery, and the syndicate has pegged me to verify what they've found. To manage the situation, if you will."

"That sounds very important," I said.

"It is. But it's far away from here. So far in fact, that I could never travel there in time. Not in this body, anyway."

"It's that far?"

"Well, I could quant there. But at that distance, there's always a risk of landing in a star or, worse, the void."

"Surely, you could travel through the gates?"

"That would still take years, and the syndicate has a sense of urgency in this matter."

"And there's no one closer?"

"The people I work for aren't too trusting."

"Thus the lace."

"Thus the lace," he said with a nod. "They tell me that once I have the neural lace, I—whatever it is that makes me I—can be backed up then sent by ansible to where the new element has been discovered."

"That's what they tell you?"

"Yeah. They told me I'd be downloaded into a new body. A duplicate of this one."

"That's true, or the plan anyway. Prospero is preparing it now—or at least working with a technician on Roxon II. The mapping we've done here is being replicated there."

"Is it like...dying?" he asked.

"Hardly," I said. "I mean, I've undergone the procedure. If anything, it's an upgrade."

"But have you ever transferred bodies? Left yours behind for another?"

I didn't want to answer this. Not many of the guests receive the procedure for travel; most receive it to interface with the Archive or some other specific tek, and of those who do, the question seldom comes up. The risk in answering is that the guest may become upset—or even unmanageable. So, rather than banter, I went right to the root of the question. "You're asking me if what defines us is separate from our bodies."

"Well," he closed his eyes tightly together to sort out the words. "Well, the idea of an entity separate from my body is so...primitive."

"How so?"

"A spirit, a deity within...dare I say—"

"A soul."

"Hrem," he cleared his throat. "A soul."

"You are a chemist. You understand the procedure. If your hand is replaced with prosthetic, are you still you?"

"Of course."

"How about your arm, or your legs, or an organ."

"Still me."

"That's all you're doing, receiving a temporary prosthetic. And, if it pleases you, we can call the you that is you whatever you like. Or we can call it a copy of what the lacework is recording. A chemical measurement and computation of your neurochemistry at any one point in time. We can call the transfer of that copy to a duplicate that's engineered down to the exact neural profile as your own...whatever you like."

"Oh," said Amory. He reclined back into the leather chaise, but appeared satisfied. "Would you look at that?"

"What's that?" I asked.

"The deep purple hue reflecting onto the lake."

"The sun will be rising soon."

His attention shifted back to me. "Your wands are gone. Is it finished?"

"Almost," I said, plucking the thimbles from each finger and placing them into an open case on my desk. "The parameters are all in place. The last of the threading is automatic. The final strands are tied at about a hundred knots per second."

"That fast?"

"Yes," I said. "That fast." From the thimble case, I removed a glass cylinder, then attached it to a fixture at the base of the sphere. I tapped the sphere. The surface of the neural lace within was iridescent and glistening in the purple mist, a web of intricately woven fractals, set in the midst of a field of stars. I twisted the end of the cylinder and the lace rolled up and slid easily inside. I opened a second case, and from the velvet lining, removed a white cylindrical tube, a wand nearly as long as my forearm. Then I removed a huge needle from the case and fastened it to the end.

"Hey," Amory said. "That's no hypo-spray."

"Hmm. No. It's not. But I assure you once more, this will not be painful. There's no need to worry. In fact, you should be watching the sunrise."

"I wish I was still sleeping."

"I woke you because I need you awake for this phase of the procedure. Now watch the sky and describe to me what you see."

"Well... It's changing rapidly. The sky is no longer deep purple, but the lake still is. The sky, on the left at any rate, I guess that's the east," he sighed deeply, "the sky to the east has become fuchsia."

"The fuchsia of sunrise is my favorite color," I said. I removed the glass lace-filled cylinder from the base of the sphere and affixed it to the end of the white tube.

"You know, I love a tangerine sunrise," said Amory. "And look there. There's a band of tangerine. It reminds me of my childhood, looking out from my parents' Mid-Hi apartment at the chemically skewed sunrise over the sprawl."

I rose from the desk and walked over to the chair to watch the sunrise by Amory's side. "Tangerine is nice too. This is one of my favorites."

"This one today?"

"This one in the Archive. There's a whole collection in there. Prospero collects rainy days, sunsets, and sunrises."

"Really? I don't suppose there's one from the Meg."

"Lilly," I said, "can we look over the East River of the NorEast Meg?"

The image beyond the wall blurred then refocused to a view of the sprawl from the Meg.

"Yes," said Amory, his voice cracking. "That's it." He leaned forward. A tear slipped down his cheek.

I placed one hand on his shoulder, and with the other, positioned the needle to the base of his skull. "This won't hurt a bit," I said. Then I squeezed the inlaid buttons on the surface of the white wand. The contents of the glass cylinder affixed to the end flushed forward and Amory's shoulders went limp. I dropped the wand to the side and, with both hands on his shoulders, swung my leg over the chaise to sit behind him.

Amory sobbed. "The sunrise is so beautiful."

"I know," I said softly, my hands gently massaging his shoulders. "I know." My gaze wasn't on the sun, but the mirror image of the neural lace unfurling of its own accord, embedding in Amory's brain.

The sun was above the trees when Amory spoke again. He was no longer sobbing, nor did he sound inebriated. "Is it complete then?"

"How do you feel?" I asked.

"I feel good. Better than good."

"Excellent," I said. I squeezed his shoulders as I lifted myself from the chaise. I picked up the white wand from the floor then returned it to its case. Then I slid my finger along the side of the sphere—rotating the image inside. "This all looks good," I said. From the top of the desk, I grabbed a small mirror and penlight. "Okay." I clicked it on and off to test it. "Now, let me have a look at you."

"Okay," he said.

I went to the front of the chaise and bent forward to inspect him.

I clicked the penlight back on. "Keep looking forward," I said, then swung the beam of the penlight back and forth from one pupil to the other. "That's good. The size of pupil is normal. Okay, follow the light to your right, good, to your left. Excellent." I held up the small mirror. "Would you like to see those blue beauties for yourself?"

"Uh. Yes," he said, taking the mirror. He held it in front of himself and opened his eyes wide. "They're such a bright blue."

"It's the dim morning light," I said, adding two large tablets to a rock glass of water. These fizzed a deep red. "And you're not used to them."

"How does the lace make them blue? Does it add pigment?"

"Quite the opposite, actually. The lace turns eyes blue by eliminating any existing pigment and reducing the melanin. You had green eyes, so there were never many pigments present in your iris or ocular fluid to begin with."

"But why blue?"

"The blue is a result of the Tyndall scattering of light in the stroma, a phenomenon similar to Rayleigh scattering, which accounts for the blueness of the sky."

"Huh." Under his breath, he rhetorically asked, "Why is the sky blue?"

"Excuse me?"

"Hrrm," he cleared his throat. "Nothing. What happens next, then?" he asked.

"Here," I said, offering him the fresh chemical cocktail. "Drink this."

Amory drank half of the mix in one gulp.

"Drink the rest," I said. And he did. Satisfied, I took the glass and placed it on my desk. "Now that the neural lace is implanted, it will grow with you. Not as quickly as it would in a child or teen, but with your age mod nanotech maintaining your system, performance will increase."

"The download, what about that?"

"I was getting to that. We now have the capability to read and store your full sentience. The you, whatever it is that makes you, you." She smiled.

He responded in kind. "So you're going to do that?"

"It's already done. We downloaded a complete scan as soon as the lace took and stored it in the archive. The process takes less than a second."

"So I'm on ice."

"On ice and in transit."

"When will I come online?"

"Soon."

"Will I be able to see myself?"

"You know the answer to that."

Amory nodded. "Due to synching," he said, "only one copy can be conscious at any time. Otherwise, all copies will become mentally unstable."

"In all but a few recorded instances," I added. "Irreversibly, and we don't want that to happen. Do we?"

"Certainly not. And where will my—this body—be kept?" he asked.

"You'll remain a guest here at the Lion's Meadow."

"I'll be in cold storage."

"Yes."

"Where exactly?"

"Beneath the lake, if you will."

"Can I see it?"

"No. I'm sorry. Guests are not permitted entry in their conscious state."

"Will I dream?"

"You, Amory, will be light years from here. On the edge of the colonies."

"And that's that. It seems like a form of euthanasia."

"Nonsense. That's what we're avoiding. In the first days, minds were forwarded to arrive before their mortal bodies. There were times those bodies didn't arrive. You will be put to sleep here, and wake up somewhere else. This body will wait for your return."

"I see. Of course. I apologize for the trepidation. It's not my nature."

"It's quite all right."

From the speakers came the sound of strings, then the tenor voice sang out, "Nessun dorma! Nessun dorma!"

"None shall sleep," I said. "Interesting choice."

"I know. It's passe'. But it was the most soothing song I could think of when I filled out the questionnaire."

I didn't mention that the song was easily the most popular chosen. Cliché would be a better description. But the tenor was beautiful and if it soothed him, all the better. "Nonsense," I said. "I adore Puccini, Turandot in particular. If you'd please, lay back down and enjoy it."

"It all happens so fast."

Outside, it was pouring, or at least that was the image presented outside of the solarium. The sky was low and the mist thick on the lake while virtual droplets gathered along the edges of the windows, merged, then ran down in streams. A tenor wailed Puccini over the sound system—Madame Butterfly, not Turandot.

The music faded. "Hi Imogen," said Prospero. "A little opera on a rainy afternoon, eh? Some things never change."

"Says the woman who just last month was an eagle."

"Some things do, and some don't," she said. "We began the resuscitation of Willinputt Beta as soon as Willinputt Alpha was placed into storage."

"Any issues?"

"No. None at all. Would you like to speak with him?"

"Yes. That would be nice."

The rain covered windows faded to black, then a brightly lit yellow room appeared outside the first story. Standing in the room, eyes piercing cerulean blue, was Amory—or at least a duplicate.

"I..." he began. "I want to thank you."

"You're welcome," I said. "It's my privilege to serve society and the syndicate."

"Yes, thank you for that. But I was referring to the sunrise. You gifted me with something I'd forgotten."

"It was your choice. Tell me. Do you feel any less—you?"

"No. No I don't," he said. A pirate smile crept across his face. "And I have you to thank for that too."

ABOUT THE AUTHORS

Michael Ezell A former US Marine and police officer, Michael now resides in Southern California with his wife, two sons, and at least five too many rescue cats.

His work has appeared in numerous anthologies, as well as *On Spec Magazine*. His short story "*The Good Food*" was selected for "The Year's Best Military and Adventure SF Vol. 3" by *Baen Books*.

He has optioned a feature film screenplay and also works in the Special Makeup Effects field as a Project Coordinator.

Will Swardstrom is a speculative fiction author. His latest novel is *Blink*, the first adventure in *The Utility Company* series, co-written with his brother Paul. He also has two full length novels, *Dead Sleep* and *Dead Sight*, and is at work on the finale in the trilogy. He also has three stories in The Future Chronicles anthology series (*Uncle Allen* in *The Alien Chronicles*, *Z Ball* in *The Z Chronicles*, and *The Control* in *The Immortality Chronicles*). Each of those anthologies has charted in the Top 5 on the SF Anthology list and The Alien Chronicles reached as high as #6 on the Overall Top 100 List. The Control from The Immortality Chronicles has been nominated for Best American Science Fiction. He also has a few stories set in Hugh Howey's WOOL Universe among his various other short stories and novellas. He lives in Southern Illinois with his wife and two kids.

Terry R. Hill is a Texas native, an aerospace engineer, has worked for NASA since 1997, and, while supporting the manned space program has been a lifetime passion, writing of different worlds, alternate futures, and the human condition has filled his spare time.

Terry is a *Kindle Worlds* Best Selling author and his post-dystopian sci-fi series *In the Days of Humans* is ranked #3 in Goodreads' list 'Amazing Books Of The 21st Century'. Terry also has published short stories, one of which is *The Journal* published in *The Future Chronicles* juggernaut *Doomsday Anthology*, in addition to *Voices from the Deep* published in *Tales from the Canyons of the Damned No. 18*.

Always looking to maximize what life has to offer, Terry has found himself singing on stage, helping to house the less fortunate, skydiving, hammering away at the Berlin Wall, wearing space suits, ice swimming in Finland in the dead of winter, bathing in the hot springs of Japan, and forging into the unknown as a parent.

Life is too short to let opportunities pass by since there is only one opportunity to ride. But mostly, it's all about the people in our everyday as we experience this thing called Life.

Jessica West (a.k.a. West1Jess) is currently pursuing a state of self-induced psychosis, also known as writing. In the past, she has worked for Wal-Mart, a lawyer, and a bank. Now if she could just get a couple years experience with the IRS and the NSA, world domination is in the bag.

Jess lives in Acadiana with three daughters still young enough to think she's cool and a husband who knows better but likes her anyway.

For more information, visit west1jess.com

Amira K. Makansi makes wine by day and worlds by night. As a traveling winemaker and full-time writer, she divides her time between working in the cellars at wineries around the world and spinning worlds into existence. In addition to the *Seeds* trilogy, Amira is hard at work on a story tentatively titled *POROUS*, a dark psychological story about a girl who can find the paths between worlds - but is being hunted by shadowy beings who threaten to destroy her entire universe.

Daniel Arthur Smith is a USA Today bestselling author. His titles include *Spectral Shift*, *Hugh Howey Lives, The Cathari Treasure*, *The Somali Deception*, and a few other novels and short stories. He also curates the phenomenal short fiction series *Tales from the Canyons of the Damned* and *Frontiers of Speculative Fiction*.

He was raised in Michigan and graduated from Western Michigan University where he studied philosophy, with focus on cognitive science, meta-physics, and comparative religion. He began his career as a bartender, barista, poetry house proprietor, teacher, and then became a technologist and futurist for the Fortune 100 across the Americas and Europe.

Daniel has traveled to over 300 cities in 22 countries, residing in Los Angeles, Kalamazoo, Prague, Crete, and now writes in Manhattan where he lives with his wife and young sons.

For more information, visit danielarthursmith.com